"You Barely Know Me. I Could Be Dangerous."

Only to her heart.

She smiled up at him. "Somehow I doubt that."

"You never know." His hands slid up to her shoulders, caressing her through the delicate, slippery silk. "I might try to take advantage of you. There's no one here to stop me."

Even in the dim light she could see flames of desire flicker in his eyes. His gaze settled on her mouth, making her lips feel swollen and warm. Her own heart began to beat double-time and her skin felt tingly and alive.

She slid her arms around his neck, pulled him close. Being in Chris's arms felt like returning home after a long arduous journey. For the first time since she was a child she felt as though she was exactly where she was supposed to be.

A rush of relief so intense washed over her that she felt like weeping. She'd never felt so vulnerable in her life, and frankly, it scared her to death.

Dear Reader,

Welcome to book five of my ROYAL SEDUCTIONS series: the story of Melissa Thornsby, the illegitimate princess of Morgan Isle, and Crown Prince Christian James Ernst Alexander of Thomas Isle.

As always, it took some time to figure these two out, to see what made them tick. And believe me, they took me on one heck of an emotional ride. Melissa thinks she's so tough, it was heart wrenching the moment she realized she didn't have all the answers. And Chris is so blind to what is right in front of him, I wanted to whack him upside the head and say, "Hello, what were you thinking?" Though it takes them both some serious soul-searching, I think you'll agree it's worth it when these two find their happily ever after.

Don't forget to watch in November for book six of my ROYAL SEDUCTIONS series and spend *Christmas with the Prince.*

Best,

Michelle

MICHELLE CELMER

ROYAL SEDUCER

Silhouette

Desire

Published by Silhouette Books
America's Publisher of Contemporary Romance

SILHOUETTE BOOKS

ISBN-13: 978-0-373-76951-3

Recycling programs
for this product may
not exist in your area.

ROYAL SEDUCER

Visit Silhouette Books at www.eHarlequin.com

Printed in U.S.A.

Books by Michelle Celmer

Silhouette Desire

Playing by the Baby Rules #1566
The Seduction Request #1626
Bedroom Secrets #1656
Round-the-Clock Temptation #1683
House Calls #1703
The Millionaire's Pregnant Mistress #1739
The Secretary's Secret #1774
Best Man's Conquest #1799
The King's Convenient Bride #1876
The Illegitimate Prince's Baby #1877
An Affair with the Princess #1900
The Duke's Boardroom Affair #1919
Royal Seducer #1951

*Royal Seductions

MICHELLE CELMER

Bestselling author Michelle Celmer lives in southeastern Michigan with her husband, their three children, two dogs and two cats. When she's not writing or busy being a mom, you can find her in the garden or curled up with a romance novel. And if you twist her arm real hard you can usually persuade her into a day of power shopping.

Michelle loves to hear from readers. Visit her Web site at www.michellecelmer.com, or write her at P.O. Box 300, Clawson, MI 48017.

To Nancy

One

Melissa Thornsby never got nervous.

She'd been raised in the pretentious and oftentimes eccentric New Orleans high society, where it wasn't all that uncommon to check one's back and occasionally find a knife or two sticking out. But that was par for the course.

After Katrina, she'd started a foundation to rebuild the city, and when she met presidents, past and present, actors, musicians and other celebrities eager to "do the right thing," it was just another day at the office.

Even when she'd learned she was the illegitimate princess of the country of Morgan Isle and made the decision to move there permanently to be with a family that was, to put it mildly, suspicious of her motives, she barely broke a sweat. She took her late mother's advice and viewed it as an adventure.

So, visiting Thomas Isle, the former rival of her native country, and meeting the royal family, really wasn't a big deal.

Until she saw *him*.

He stood on the tarmac of the small private airstrip in the bright afternoon sunshine, flanked by two very frightening-looking bodyguards and a polished black Bentley at the ready. And he was, for lack of a better word, *beautiful*. Tall, fit and well put together in a tailored, charcoal-gray pinstriped suit.

Prince Christian James Ernst Alexander, next in line to the throne of Thomas Isle. Confirmed bachelor and shameless playboy. His photos didn't do him justice.

She descended the steps of the Learjet and the prince approached, flashing her a million-watt stunner of a smile. Her heart leapt up into her throat and a curious tickle of nerves coiled in her belly. Was it too much to hope that he was to be her guide for the duration of her two-week stay? Although in her experience that task was typically left up to the princess since the crown prince was usually busy with slightly more significant tasks, such as preparing to run the entire country.

Flanked by her own equally threatening entourage—the security detail her half brother, King Phillip, insisted she have accompany her—she stepped forward to meet him halfway.

When they were face to face, he nodded his head in

greeting and said, in a voice as rich and as smooth as her favorite gourmet dark chocolate, "Welcome to Thomas Isle, Your Highness."

"Your Highness." She dipped into a curtsey, turning on the Southern-belle charm. "It's an honor to be here."

"The honor is all ours," he said with a lethal smile. Lethal because she could feel it, like a buzz of pure energy, from the roots of her hair to the balls of her feet.

He watched her intently with eyes a striking shade of green, and behind them she could see very clearly a hint of mischief and sly determination. She couldn't help wondering if he'd spent his previous life as a cat.

He noted her security detail and with one brow slightly raised, asked, "Expecting a revolution, Your Highness?"

Nodding to his own "muscle," she answered, "I was going to ask you the same thing."

If the question had been some sort of test, she could see that she'd passed. He grinned, playful and sexy, and the coil of nerves in her gut twisted into a hopeless knot. This really wasn't like her at all. Heaven knows, she was used to men flirting with her. Young and old, rich and poor, and all of them after the ludicrous trust her great-aunt and uncle had left her. But somehow, she didn't think the prince had money on his mind. He was one of the few men she'd met whose wealth exceeded her own. At least, she was assuming it did.

"The bodyguards were King Phillip's idea," she told him.

"Of course, you're welcome to keep them with you," he said, "but it's certainly not necessary."

Phillip had insisted she take the bodyguards with her, but he never said she had to *keep* them there. And call her optimistic, but entrusting her welfare to Prince Christian's staff seemed to her a valuable gesture of good faith. In the vast, stormy history of their two countries, the peace they had adopted was for all practical purposes still in its infancy. And her duty, the way she saw it, was to build on that.

"You'll see that they're flown back safely?" she asked.

He nodded. "Of course, Your Highness."

She cringed inwardly. She still hadn't grown used to the royal title. "Please, call me Melissa."

"Melissa," he said, with that sexy British accent. "I like that."

And she liked the way he said it.

"You can call me Chris. I imagine it best we drop the formalities, seeing as we will be spending a considerable amount of time together the next two weeks."

Would they? Another jolt of nerves sizzled inside her stomach. "Are you to be my guide?" she asked.

"If you're agreeable," he said.

As though she would say *no* to two weeks with a gorgeous and charming prince. She smiled and said, "I look forward to it."

He gestured to the waiting car. "Shall we go?"

She turned to her bodyguards, dismissing them with a simple, "Thank you, gentlemen."

They exchanged an uneasy glance, but remained silent. They knew as well as she did that Phillip would not be happy she'd sent them home.

Oh, well. If there was one thing her new family had learned, it was that she had a mind of her own. As deeply as she longed to be accepted as one of them, to have a real family for the first time since losing her parents, there was only so much of herself she was willing to sacrifice. At thirty-three, in many respects she was too set in her ways to change.

The prince touched her elbow to lead her to the car, and despite the layers of silk and linen of her suit jacket, her skin simmered with warmth. When was the last time she'd felt such a sizzling connection to a man? Or perhaps the better question was, when was the last time she'd let herself? This was as much vacation as business, and it wouldn't hurt to let her hair down and have some fun.

He helped her into the back, and she sank into the rich, butter-soft leather seat. He circled the car and climbed in the opposite side, filling the interior with a warm and delicious scent that left her feeling light-headed. Were she home, she might have blamed it on the Southern heat, but the temperature here hadn't even topped eighty degrees and there was no humidity to speak of. Warm for mid-June on Thomas Isle, but mild by her standards.

As soon as the doors were closed they were off in the direction of the castle, which couldn't be more than a few minutes away, as they had flown past it just before landing. It appeared massive from the air—dare she say larger than the much more modern palace on Morgan Isle—and seemed to have acres of emerald-green lawns, ornately patterned gardens, and even a shrubbery maze.

A passionate lover of nature, she could hardly wait to explore it all. Her mother had been an avid gardener. Melissa's childhood home on Morgan Isle was renowned for its award-winning gardens, and she'd carried on the tradition at her own estate in New Orleans. Though it had been hard to leave that and move back to Morgan Isle, the U.S. had never really been her home. Since losing her parents, she had never felt as though she truly belonged anywhere.

"My parents, the king and queen, are anxious to meet you," Chris said.

"The feeling is mutual." She turned to him and realized he was studying her, a curious look on his face. "What?"

"Your accent," he said. "I can't quite place it."

"That's because it's a mishmash of different dialects. Little bits of every place I've lived pop out occasionally."

"How many different places have you lived?"

"Let's see…" she counted off on her fingers. "I lived on Morgan Isle until I was ten, then I relocated to New Orleans, then it was off to boarding school in France and summers in California, then college on the east coast, then back to New Orleans."

"Sounds exciting," he said.

One would think so, but really all she had ever wanted was to settle down, stay in one place. Of course, when she finally had, it just hadn't felt...right. She'd thought that moving back to Morgan Isle would give her the sense of home and family she had been longing for, but she'd been disappointed to find that despite it being her true home, she still felt like an outsider. It left her wondering if she would ever fit in anywhere.

"How about you?" she asked the prince.

"My diplomatic travels have taken me all over the world, but I've never lived anywhere but here, with my family."

She detected a vague note of exasperation in his tone. To her it sounded wonderful. After her parents died, she had been shuttled to the States to live with her great-aunt and uncle, who had little concept of family. Childless by choice, they saw their orphaned great-niece as more of an interloper than a part of the family. They wasted little time shipping her off to boarding school for her education and camp for the summers. Not that she blamed them. They'd done the best they could. Had they chosen not to take her in she would have become a ward of the state, and who knows where she would be today.

Melissa became aware that the car was climbing, and she knew that they were nearly there. Then the trees cleared and there sat the royal castle, like a scene from a child's picture book, high on a cliff overlooking the ocean and hovering like a sentinel above a charming village below. Far less modern than Morgan Isle, she thought with a tug of pride, but magnificent nonetheless.

She felt a little as though she had been thrown back into a past century.

From what she'd learned in her research, where Morgan Isle was modern and forward-thinking—a flourishing and expanding resort community—Thomas Isle was traditional and private. Most of their economy was based on export, primarily fishing and organic farming. Some considered it archaic, but she saw it as quaint and charming.

"It's magnificent," she told him, gazing up from the car window.

"Do you know the history between our two countries?"

"Only that they've been rivals for many years."

"It's a fascinating story. Were you aware that both islands used to be ruled by one family? A king and queen with two sons. Twins, born only minutes apart."

"Their names wouldn't have been Thomas and Morgan, would they?"

He smiled. "In fact, they were. When the king died, the princes became ensnared in a battle over who would be become the next ruler. They each felt they deserved the title. When an accord couldn't be reached, one challenged the other to a duel." He paused for dramatic effect. "To the death.

"The survivor would reign as king. But their mother couldn't bear the thought of losing either one of them, and begged them not to fight. She suggested a compromise. They could split the kingdom by each taking one of the islands. They agreed, but their discord was so bitter, they never spoke again."

"That's so sad."

"To spite the other, each chose his own name for his island. Their subjects, as a show of loyalty to their respective kings, were banned from visiting the island on which they didn't reside, or even communicating with its people. Many families were broken and businesses ruined."

"What about the queen? Which island did she choose?"

"She refused to choose between her sons and was banished from both islands."

She pressed a hand to her heart. "Oh, my goodness, how awful!" How could they banish their own mother?

"It took hundreds of years to put our history behind us," he said. "That's why it's so important that we maintain accord between our two countries. Joining our resources could benefit both our islands. Both of our societies. Both of our families."

"King Phillip feels the same way," she assured him. "That's why I'm here."

"I'm relieved to hear that. Matters such as these have the potential to be very…awkward."

"I'm a go-with-the-flow princess," she said, which was true, for the most part. "However, I take my new role very seriously. Anything for the good of the country."

He flashed her another one of those sizzling smiles. "Then I'm sure we'll get along quite well."

The car pulled up the drive to the gates, where a mob of press waited with microphones poised and cameras at the ready.

The gates swung open and guards in formal uniform

stepped forward to control the crowd. The car continued on past a stone wall that seemed to extend miles in
each direction, and what she saw on the other side took
her breath away. Everything looked green and vibrant,
and the castle itself was a towering edifice of stone and
mortar and ornate stained-glass windows, all meticulously maintained and preserved.

"Welcome to Sparrowfax Castle," Chris said.

It was clear, as they rounded the drive and she saw
the royal family and what appeared to be the entire staff
lined up awaiting their arrival, that they were pulling out
all of the royal stops. That annoying knot of nerves
coiled even tighter in her belly.

This sure seemed liked a lot of trouble to go to for a
simple diplomatic visit. Yet she couldn't let herself
forget how important this was to her family and country,
which would mean watching her behavior. Particularly
biting her sharp Southern tongue that sometimes had a
mind of its own.

As the car slowed to a halt, footmen in royal dress
approached to open the doors. Melissa took the prof-
fered hand thrust her way and rose from the back seat,
feeling underdressed in her basic linen suit. The family
was dressed and poised to receive royalty—which she
had to remind herself, *she was*—and for the first time
in her adult life she felt apprehensive about her suitability.

Chris's parents, the king and queen, stepped forward
to greet her. Though getting up in years, they appeared

healthy and vibrant. Their other children, Chris's brother and twin sisters, were as breathtakingly attractive as their sibling. What a privilege it would be, Melissa mused, to belong to such a beautiful family. It was a wonder that all of them had yet to marry.

Good looks, however, were only a fraction of a much larger picture. For all she knew they could be rude and unfriendly.

Chris appeared at her side, and though it was silly, his presence seemed to have a calming effect on her.

"All this for me?" she asked.

Her question seemed to perplex him. "Of course. You're an honored guest. Your visit marks a new era for both of our kingdoms."

Little ol' me? She hadn't realized her visit would be seen as quite that big of a deal. Her own family hadn't put up close to this much fuss when she'd come home to her native land. In fact, there hadn't been any fuss at all. Her return to Morgan Isle had been very hush-hush, to avoid a media frenzy.

But it wasn't as though she was going to complain. What woman didn't enjoy a little ego-stroking every now and then?

Chris offered his arm. "Are you ready to meet my family?"

She looped her arm through his, finding his solid warmth a decadent treat. And a comfort. He made her feel…safe.

She smiled up at him and nodded. Back in New

Orleans she sat at the very top of the social food chain. But none of that carried much weight here, where she was known only as the illegitimate daughter of the late King Frederick.

And she suspected that for the rest of her life no one would let her forget it.

Two

Within five minutes of meeting her, Chris suspected that he and Princess Melissa would get along quite well.

Though he typically preferred blondes, Melissa's dark hair and eyes and her warm complexion were unexpectedly exotic and appealing. She was not only attractive and seemingly pleasant, but as had been suggested by King Phillip, she had a resilient personality and a sharp wit. Traits some might find undesirable, but a necessity for the type of arrangement they were considering.

He walked her over to his family to start the introductions. It had already been determined how everyone was to behave. It was imperative they make her feel welcome.

"Melissa, I would like to introduce you to my parents, the king and queen of Thomas Isle."

Melissa curtsied and said, "It's an honor, Your Majesties."

His mother took her hand and said warmly, "The honor is ours, Melissa. We're so happy that you could visit us."

"I hope we find it mutually beneficial," his father said, his tone serious.

"I'm certain we will," Melissa answered with a warm smile.

The king cast Chris a sideways glance, one that conveyed the message *don't screw this up*. Despite his past resistance when it came to the idea of settling down, even Chris couldn't deny that an alliance with the royals of Morgan Isle would be a smart move. Politically and financially.

"Meet my brother and sisters," Chris said, introducing them each in turn. "Prince Aaron Felix Gastel, and princesses Anne Charlotte Amalia and Louisa Josephine Elisabeth."

"It's a pleasure to meet you all," Melissa said. She shook each of their hands, and just as planned, they all greeted her warmly. Aaron was simply relieved that it was Chris in this position and not himself, though at thirty-one he should have been ready for the responsibility.

Louisa, the younger fraternal twin by five minutes, greeted Melissa with her usual bubbly enthusiasm. From the time that she was a small child, Louisa loved everyone, often to her own detriment. Her siblings had spent a good deal of time sheltering her from harm.

Anne was the older and more cautious twin. Too many times her trust had been betrayed by people she had mistakenly considered her friends. But even she put her best foot forward and welcomed Melissa warmly. She, like everyone else, knew how important it was that this visit go smoothly.

The introductions complete, Chris gestured to the maid who would tend to Melissa for the duration of her trip.

"Elise, would you please show our guest to her quarters?" Then he asked Melissa, "How much time do you need to settle in?"

"Not long," she said, a light of excitement flashing in the dark depths of her eyes. "I'm anxious to see the gardens. They looked decadent from the air."

"Then that's where we'll begin," he told her. "Will an hour suffice?"

She nodded. "I'll expect you in an hour."

Elise stepped forward, curtsied, and said, "This way, Your Highness."

When they disappeared inside the castle and out of earshot, and the staff was dismissed to resume their duties, everyone seemed to let out a collective breath of relief.

"I think that went quite well," his mother said.

And from his father, "Have you discussed it with her?"

Chris refrained from rolling his eyes and struggled to keep the exasperation from his voice. "Of course not, Father. We've only just met."

His mother shot her husband a sharp look. "Give it time, James." Then she told Chris, "Take all the time you need, dear. A decision like this shouldn't be rushed. But I do have to say, I think she's lovely."

"Although illegitimate," the king reminded her.

"That's hardly her fault," she snapped back. "Besides, what family doesn't have its share of scandal? And *secrets*."

"Just some more than others," Aaron quipped, receiving a stern look from the his mother.

"Well, I like her," Louisa bubbled.

Anne shot her an exasperated look. "You like *everyone*."

"Not *everyone*. But I really like Melissa, and I'm an excellent judge of character."

Actually, Louisa was a rotten judge of character, but Chris hoped in this case she was right.

"We all have to remember to be on our best behavior," their mother said firmly. "Make her feel welcome." She took Chris's hands in hers and gave them a squeeze. "I think this might be the one, dear."

Though at first he had resisted, now Chris was inclined to agree.

He was quite sure already that Melissa would make a suitable wife.

"We need to talk," Aaron said quietly to Chris as the rest of the family dispersed.

Chris nodded and followed his brother away from the castle, where they could speak in private. "Is there a problem?"

"There might be," Aaron said, brow wrinkled with concern, which wasn't at all like him. It took a lot to put a frown on his face.

"Something about Melissa?"

Aaron shook his head. "No, no, nothing like that. I had an urgent message from the foreman of the east fields, saying he needed to see me as soon as possible. So I drove down there this morning."

The east fields, which made up close to a third of the royal family's vast acreage, was used primarily to grow soy and housed the largest of their research and greenhouse facilities. "What did he want?"

"There's some sort of disease causing a blight on the crops. A strain he doesn't recognize."

Due to the organic nature of their business, disease and insect infestations were at times a concern. "Is it treatable?"

"He's tried several methods, but so far it appears resistant. He called in a botanist from the university who he believes will be able to help. But at the rate it's spreading, we could lose half of the crop. Maybe more."

Which would be unfortunate, but not a devastating loss. Unless it spread. "You say it's confined to the east fields?"

"So far, yes."

"And there have been no problems reported from local farmers?"

"None that I've heard."

"Good. Lets try to keep it that way. The last thing we

need right now is an epidemic. Or the fear of one." Which could be just as damaging. The timing couldn't be worse. "And we shouldn't burden Father with this. Not until it's absolutely necessary."

"I'll see that the situation is handled discreetly," Aaron assured him. "Although if it begins to spread we'll have no choice but to post a countrywide bulletin."

"Let's hope it doesn't come to that." This alliance with the royal family of Morgan Isle depended on a stable economy and strong leadership. Their father's health issues were a closely guarded secret known only to the family and the king's personal physician. And Chris intended to keep it that way. If he was to become king, sooner rather than later as the case might be, he needed a strong base on which to build.

"Try not to worry about it. Concentrate on your princess." Aaron flashed Chris a sly grin. "Not that it will be much of a hardship. She's very attractive."

"And just think, once I'm married off, you'll be next."

Aaron snorted out a rueful laugh. "I wouldn't hold your breath. Only the crown prince is required to marry and have an heir."

"That won't stop Mother from setting you up with every eligible female on the island."

"She knows better."

Chris laughed and said, "You keep telling yourself that. But mark my words, the instant I'm spoken for, you'll be next."

Aaron glared at him. "Don't you have a princess to seduce?"

He did, and seduce her was exactly what he planned to do.

The interior of the castle was even more magnificent than the exterior.

As the maid led Melissa up to the room she would occupy for the duration of her visit, she took in with sheer wonder the high, ornately scribed ceilings and tall stained-glass windows, the authentic period furniture, magnificent tapestries and rich oriental rugs over gleaming polished wood and inlaid marble floors. On the walls hung amazing works of art, landscapes and portraits and even a few abstracts.

In New Orleans she'd seen many magnificent residences—her own estate had been highlighted in its share of newspaper and magazine articles—and the palace on Morgan Isle was the pinnacle of luxury and style. Yet none could compare to the grandeur of Sparrowfax Castle. Though she had anticipated a dark, dank atmosphere—it was after all built of stone and mortar—it was surprisingly bright and airy, her own room included.

While her things were unpacked, she took some time to change and freshen her makeup, then investigate her chamber. It wasn't a terribly large room, maybe only a third the size of her suite at the palace. But what it lacked in size, it made up for in luxury. The furnishings were rich and traditional, authentic to the period and meticulously preserved.

The bathroom was enormous and updated with all the modern amenities, including a whirlpool tub and three-headed shower. The stall, she noticed, was big enough for two. And she was sure that as good as Chris looked in his clothes, he probably looked better out of them.

Don't get ahead of yourself, Mel.

She unpacked her laptop, booted it up, and typed in her password, scanning for a wireless signal. Her family expected daily updates on her visit and trusted encrypted e-mails over a cellular line that could easily be intercepted. Not that Mel expected they would be doing espionage, but she supposed one could never be too careful.

She established a link and opened her e-mail program, addressing a note to Phillip. She wrote:

Arrived safely. Greeted warmly. Nothing to report yet.

A knock sounded at her door, so she hit Send and snapped her laptop shut. She crossed the room and opened the door.

Chris stood on the other side. He had changed out of his suit into dark slacks and a black silk dress shirt.

He looked delicious. Dark and sexy and a little mysterious.

"I hope I'm not interrupting," he said.

"Of course not." She flashed him a warm smile, and

noticed the way his eyes roamed slowly over her with no shame or hesitation, taking in the gauzy silk dress she had changed into. The deep, warm blue enhanced the gray of her eyes. She'd also let her hair down and brushed it out until it hung in rich, dark waves down her back.

She looked damned good, and it didn't go unnoticed.

"You look lovely," he said, heat flickering in the depths of his eyes like emerald flames. "How fortunate I am to have the privilege of spending the next two weeks with such a beautiful woman."

His words made her feel weak in the knees, and she was tempted to say *You're not so shabby yourself.* But she should at least play a little hard to get. Instead she batted her lashes and turned on the Southern charm. "You flatter me, Your Highness."

He grinned like a sly, hungry wolf anticipating his next meal. And, oh, how she hoped he would sink those pearly whites into her.

"Is the room satisfactory?" he asked.

"Quite," she said. "What I've seen of the castle is breathtaking."

"Are you ready to see the gardens?"

More than he could imagine. "I'd love to."

He offered his arm for her to take, and she slid hers through it. Again she felt that exciting little rush of awareness. That tingle of attraction. And she could tell by the heat in his gaze that he felt it, too.

He led her downstairs, gesturing to points of interest along the way. Family heirlooms that dated back hundreds of years, gifted to the royal family from friends and relatives and neighboring kingdoms. Melissa had so little left of her own family. After her mother and the man she'd known as her father had been killed, her aunt and uncle had seen that all of their possessions had been auctioned off and the proceeds put in a trust. But Mel would have preferred their possessions, something to remember them by, more than all the money in the world.

She didn't even have the albums of photographs and scrapbooks her mother had meticulously kept. They had probably been tossed in the trash, deemed useless. The only reminder Melissa had of her parents was a single 4x6 snapshot of the three of them taken only weeks before their accident.

"It must be wonderful to be so connected to your family," she said. "To be so close."

He shrugged. "It all depends on how you look at it, I suppose."

"Well, it looks pretty good to me." She had hoped to rediscover that closeness, that sense of continuity with her half siblings, yet something was missing. Though they made an effort to include her, she still felt like an outsider. And maybe she always would.

She was the oldest, and illegitimate or not, technically, she had a rightful claim to the crown. But despite signing documents swearing that she would never challenge Phillip's position as ruler, she didn't think they were ready to trust her. Maybe someday.

Then again, maybe not.

Chris led her through an enormous great room and out a rear door onto a slate patio bordered by a meticulously tended perennial garden so alive with color its beauty made her gasp.

"It's amazing," she said. On the patio sat a variety of chairs, chaise longues and wrought-iron tables. She could just imagine herself out there in the morning, drinking coffee, or lounging in the afternoon, reading a book. She closed her eyes and breathed in the salty tang of ocean air, could hear the waves in the distance, lapping against the rocky bluff.

It felt like paradise.

"Do you spend much time out here?" she asked him.

He shook his head. "It's mostly used for entertaining. Although you might occasionally find Louisa out here practicing yoga."

If she lived in the castle, Melissa would be out here every day, weather permitting. Although that was easy to say. She hadn't spent nearly as much time as she would have liked in her gardens at her New Orleans estate. There always seemed to be more pressing business that needed tending.

"Can we walk to the bluff?" she asked.

"Of course." He offered his arm and they walked down a twisting sandstone path that wound its way through the gardens. His knowledge of the different varieties of flowers and shrubs impressed her, as did the steady strength of his arm, and his solid presence beside her.

She'd never been what one would consider a fading flower, she could hold her own in almost any given situation, but even she liked to be pampered every now and then.

"Can I ask you a personal question, Melissa?"

She didn't have to wait for the question to know what was on his mind. She could hear it in his tone, see the curiosity in his eyes.

She'd been getting that same look from many people lately.

"Let me guess. You're wondering if it was a shock to learn that I was an illegitimate royal?"

He grinned. "Something like that."

Her illegitimacy wasn't something Melissa tried to hide, or felt she should be ashamed of. After all, how could she be responsible for the actions of a mother she'd lost twenty-three years ago, and a father she had never even known? Nor was she shy about discussing it. Why attempt to hide something everyone already knew? It would only sit like the proverbial elephant in the room. She was who she was, and people either accepted her or they didn't. Loved her or hated her.

"I felt as though I'd been caught up in some surreal sequel to *The Princess Diaries*," she said.

His eyes crinkled with confusion. *"Princess Diaries?"*

"Suffice it to say, I was flabbergasted. I had no idea that I wasn't my father's daughter."

"Did it upset you that your parents never told you the truth?"

"On some level. But honestly, I have little room to

complain. If my father knew I wasn't his, he never let it show. I had an extremely happy childhood. And my real father…well, I honestly think he did me a favor by staying out of my life. Although after my parents died it would have been nice if he'd claimed me. But I understand why he didn't."

"Life after your parents passed away wasn't so happy?"

The directness of his question surprised her a bit. Most people tiptoed around the subject of her parents' deaths. It seemed almost as though he was testing her. Seeing how tough she was.

"To quote Nietzsche," she said "'That which does not kill me makes me stronger.'"

Chris smiled. "I believe he also said, 'No price is too high to pay for the privilege of owning yourself'."

And she did own herself. Despite everything that had happened, she was in control of her own life. Her own destiny. And she intended to keep it that way.

The path ended and the gardens opened up to a rocky bluff that seemed to stretch for miles in either direction. Over its edge was nothing but cloudless sky and calm blue ocean, and farther in the distance, the coast of Morgan Isle. Fishing boats dotted the expanse that lay between the two islands, and closer to the Morgan Isle shore she could just make out the luxury craft common to the tourist trade.

She toed closer to the edge and peeked over the side, to the jagged rocks below. It was a *long* way down. At least three or four stories, with no discernible beach that she could make out in either direction. She looked back at Chris. "Is there a path down?"

He shook his head. "Not for miles. It's a straight drop down to the water. Tactically speaking, it was the perfect place for my ancestors to build the castle. Invading forces would have been forced to dock their ships miles down the coast."

She leaned farther over, trying to see the sharp incline of the cliff wall.

"Be careful," he said, concern in his voice.

"I'm always careful." At least, *almost* always.

"Not afraid of heights, I guess."

She shrugged and backed away from the edge. "Not afraid of anything, really."

He regarded her curiously. "Everyone is afraid of *something*."

She though about it for a moment, then said, "Centipedes."

He grinned. "Centipedes?"

"All those legs." She shuddered. "They give me a serious case of the creeps."

"Well, then, you have nothing to fear here," he said, offering his arm and leading her back toward the castle. "We don't see many centipedes."

There was one other thing she feared. Feared it more than a stampede of creepy centipedes.

She was afraid she might fall for Prince Christian. Then get her heart broken as she had so many times before.

Three

Chris and Melissa strolled slowly back to the castle, she a soft and comfortable presence beside him. They chatted about the weather and the flowers and the different crops they grew on the island. She had an insatiable curiosity about practically everything, and always looked genuinely interested in his answers and explanations. But when he led her past the shrubbery maze, her eyes all but shimmered with excitement. She stopped him just outside the entrance. "It's taller than it looks from the air."

"Three meters, give or take," Chris said. "It takes an entire crew a full day to manicure."

"I'm sure it's worth it."

"This maze has been standing here, unchanged, for hundreds of years."

Her eyes filled with mischief. "Could we go inside?"

"You'd like me to lead you through?"

"Oh, no, I'll figure it out myself."

Chris looked at his watch. "Unfortunately, there's no time. We're to meet with my parents for drinks before supper."

"How long does it usually take?"

"Drinks or supper?"

She laughed. "No, the maze."

"If you know your way, not long. Ten minutes, maybe. For the novice, though, it's easy to get turned around. I've seen people wander through there for hours."

She shot him a cocky smile. "I'll bet I could figure it out in no time."

"It's more confusing than you might think."

"I have a very good sense of direction. And I like a challenge."

He didn't doubt that she did. She certainly had spunk. He liked that about her. In his opinion, it took a strong and independent woman to withstand a marriage of convenience. Melissa seemed to have what it would take. He hoped she felt the same way.

"Just in case, I think it should wait."

She looked disappointed, but she didn't push the issue. Duty was duty, and she seemed to embrace the concept. One more trait in her favor.

"Tomorrow, then?" she asked.

"Of course."

She gazed up at him through a curtain of thick, dark lashes, a wicked smile teasing the corners of her lips. "You promise?"

"I'm a man of my word," he said.

"I'm sure you've heard the saying 'Chivalry is dead.'"

"Not on Morgan Isle it isn't." He gazed down at her, into the smoky depths of her eyes, and swore he could see a shadow of apprehension. Maybe even sorrow. Then it was gone.

Either he'd imagined it, or she wasn't as tough as she wanted people to believe.

"Now," he said, "are you ready to have drinks with my parents?"

"I guess so." She took a long, deep breath, and blew it out. Then asked, "Anything I should know beforehand? It's important that I make a good impression."

"Just be yourself and I know they'll find you as enchanting and interesting as I do."

He could see from her smile that she appreciated his answer.

"I like you, Your Highness."

He returned the smile. "I would have to say, that's a very good thing."

"Why is that?"

"Because, Princess, I like you, too."

As Melissa had suspected, "drinks with the king and queen" was code for a thorough grilling by not only Chris's parents, but his brother and sisters as well. They seemed to want to know all about her and her half siblings, and the country of Morgan Isle. And they weren't shy about asking. She tried to answer their questions as honestly as possible without giving away too much, or in some cases, too little. She had been with her new family such a short time that in some cases she simply didn't know the answers.

Dinner was a five-course feast of seafood caught off their own shores, organic vegetables from the royal family's personal garden and bread baked fresh from wheat grown in their own fields. They followed it up with a dessert that was so mouthwateringly delicious Melissa was tempted to ask for seconds.

Though she had never been one to choose organic or natural products, it really did make a difference. She would go so far as to say it was one of the tastiest, freshest meals she'd ever eaten.

It was nine-thirty by the time dinner was over and she thoroughly expected another round of drinks, and very possibly more questions. Instead, Chris's parents excused themselves to their quarters. The king did look exhausted, but she supposed that was only natural when she considered that he spent his days running an entire country. And though he didn't exactly have one foot in the grave, he was no kid, either. In his late sixties would be her guess, but she wasn't rude enough to ask.

She also didn't miss the way his children seemed to coddle him. The fleeting and furtive looks of concern they would direct his way when they thought no one was looking. She couldn't escape the feeling that there was something going on with his royal highness. Something they didn't want her to know.

Everyone said their good-nights, his brother and sisters included—although she doubted they all actually went to bed this early—and Chris walked her to her room.

"Everyone retires early here," she said when they stopped outside her door.

He leaned against the doorjamb. "Our primary business is farming. Early to bed, early to rise."

"In New Orleans, if I was in bed by one it was an early night. It's a totally different culture."

"To be honest," he said, "I've always been something of a night owl myself."

"Would you like to come in for a while?" she asked, gesturing inside her room. "We could have a drink and…talk."

He looked past her into the bedroom. A single lamp burned beside the bed and the maid had turned down the covers. There was no denying that it looked awfully inviting. "I'd like to, but I shouldn't."

"Tired of me already?" she teased.

"Quite the opposite." He took a step closer, his eyes simmering with desire. "If I allow myself to come into your room tonight, you know as well as I that we'll be doing much more than just talking. Is that what you want?"

Though a part of her wanted to say *yes*—the curious, reckless, and let's face it, *lonely* part—she knew it wouldn't be right. She'd met him only a few hours ago.

Shouldn't she at least get to know him a little before she let her hormones call the shots? Before she gave in to the inevitable? Because she knew without a doubt that sometime before she flew home to Morgan Isle, she would sleep with Chris.

But not tonight.

"No, I guess not." She took a step back from him, from the heady pull of attraction that would instead have her wrapping her arms around his neck and pulling him closer for a long, deep kiss.

He looked disappointed, but not at all surprised. "I thought we would take a tour of the island tomorrow. See the village and the fields we control."

She smiled. "I'd like that."

"Shall we have breakfast first? Say, eight o'clock. If that's not too early."

She doubted she'd be able to sleep late, if she slept at all. She smiled. "I'd like that."

"Good night, Melissa. Sleep well."

"Good night, Chris."

He took her hand in his and lifted it to his lips, brushing a soft kiss against it, and for an instant she thought he might take her in his arms and kiss her anyway, then he let go of her hand and backed away. He flashed her one last dark, sizzling smile, then disappeared down the hallway.

She closed the door and leaned against it.

Wow.

Her heart pounded and she felt drunk on the sensation of his lips against her skin. If she did sleep, she had no doubt whatsoever that she would dream of him.

She changed into her favorite silk nightgown—which also happened to be her sexiest, since one never knew—and because she wasn't the least bit sleepy, booted up her laptop to check her e-mail.

There was one from Phillip. It said simply:

Have you spoken with the king and queen?

No *How was your trip,* or *Are you having fun?* He didn't even ask why she'd sent the bodyguards home.

She couldn't help but feel he was relieved that she was gone. Which could very well be her imagination. Phillip was not what anyone could call warm and fuzzy. He was, she imagined, very much like their father. With the exception of his sleeping habits.

As in, Phillip was faithful to his wife, while their father, it seemed, hadn't been able to keep it in his pants.

She hit Reply and typed up a quick e-mail, giving Phillip a brief rundown on her visit so far. Leaving out the part about almost shacking up with Prince Christian. Phillip wanted her to become well acquainted with the royal family of Thomas Isle, particularly their future leader, but she didn't think he meant *that* well.

She'd never been one to sleep around, though that was not to say she was a prude in any respect, but maybe there was more of her father in her than she cared to admit.

She sent the e-mail and, with nothing better to do, opened her favorite card game, but after fifteen minutes or so was bored to tears. She tried curling up in bed and reading the book she'd brought along with her, but she couldn't concentrate.

She called down to the kitchen for a cup of herbal tea, but not even that would quiet her nerves. Back home in New Orleans, a stroll in the garden under the moon and the stars was usually the most effective cure for a sleepless night. She doubted anyone would mind if she took a quick walk. Besides, how would they even know? Unlike her, they were all soundly sleeping.

She slipped on her robe and opened her door, peering out into the hall. In the palace on Morgan Isle, it seemed there was always some sort of activity going on, day or night, whether it was midnight bottle feedings or diaper changes, or the guards' nightly rounds of the premises. In contrast, the castle was quiet and dark.

Melissa stepped into the hall and quietly made her way down the stairs and through the castle to the patio door. She slipped outside onto the patio, the slate smooth against her bare feet. The air was cool and damp, and the full moon cast a silver, ghostly glow across the land. In the distance she could hear the *whoosh* of the ocean against the bluff, but otherwise the night was eerily still.

To the east, just beyond the garden, stood the shrubbery maze, looking ominous in the dark. Yet it seemed to beckon her. If it was a challenge during the day, think of the thrill it would be to guess her way through with only the moon to light her way.

She glanced back at the castle, dark and still, and figured, *why the heck not?* This was supposed to be a vacation. And what was the worst that could happen? She would get lost and wander around in there all night.

She stepped off the patio onto the cool, damp grass and cut across the lawn to the entrance of the maze, her heart thumping a little faster with excitement.

Here goes nothin'.

She stepped forward and the maze swallowed her into its depths like a hungry animal. Inside it was dark and serene, and the towering greenery seemed to muffle all sound beyond its walls.

She waited for her eyes to adjust, until she could see the first turn ahead of her. She stepped forward, deeper inside, the grass cool and slippery under her feet. She turned the first corner to find herself at the end of a long, ominous-looking passageway. Memorizing her steps in case she needed to back her way out later, she walked slowly forward. Halfway through she encountered another passageway that hooked off to the right. Should she maintain her present course, or turn down a path that would take her deeper inside?

The adventurer in her said go deeper.

She turned and followed the passage, but after a few yards she reached a T in the path. Should she go right, or left? Logic dictated that turning right would put her on course for a dead end, so she went left instead.

Behind her she swore she heard a rustling, but when she turned to look, there was nothing there. Probably just a bat, or some small animal. She shrugged and continued on through a few more twists and turns until she reached another T. This time she chose right. She heard another noise, a distinct rustling of branches, but this time it seemed to be coming from in front of her. She strained to see in the dim light, and could swear she saw a dark figure cross the path somewhere in front of her.

Her imagination? A trick of the light?

Curious, she forged ahead, turning the same direction as the figure had, and found herself at a dead end. There wasn't anyone or anything there.

That was odd. She felt around, looking for some sort of secret passage. There was nothing but solid branches, far too thick and brittle to slip through. Then she heard the rustling again, this time from directly behind her.

She spun around, but there was no one there. Yet she had the distinct feeling she wasn't alone. "Hello?" she called. "Is someone there?"

There was another rustle, then the dark figure passed the T junction just ahead of her. It was too dark to tell who it was, or even if it was a man or a woman.

She darted after the ghostly figure, determined to catch up. But it seemed as though no matter how swiftly she moved, he or she was always rounding the next corner, out of sight before she could get very close. Whoever it was, they obviously knew the maze well. They had lured Melissa deep inside, and she'd been concentrating so hard on following him or her, she hadn't been memorizing her steps. Now she had no idea how to get out.

She suspected that had been the intention all along.

Whoever it was, he was taunting her. Trying to throw her off track, and it had worked. She was hopelessly turned around. And of course, her ghostly figure had chosen that moment to disappear without a trace.

"Swell," she mumbled to herself. She wandered around for another twenty minutes or so trying to get her bearings, hearing an occasional rustle in the leaves, sometimes in front of her, sometimes behind. If this was some sort of test, she was failing miserably. She strained to hear the ocean, to get a bearing on her direction, but it was useless, and since the idea of wandering around in there all night held little to no appeal, she threw in the towel.

"You win," she called. "I surrender."

"I told you it was confusing," a voice said softly into her ear.

She spun around and crashed into the wall of one very long, solid and—oh, Lord—blissfully bare chest.

Chris's chest.

Four

Melissa was so surprised she nearly toppled over backward. Chris grabbed her arms to steady her, the heat of his hands searing her through the thin silk of her robe. He wore a playful, slightly cocky grin that she felt all the way through to the center of her bones.

"What are you doing out here?" she asked.

"I was just about to ask you the same thing."

"I couldn't sleep. I decided to go for a walk."

"In the middle of the night?" His eyes raked over her and the gentle pressure on her arms increased. "In your night clothes?"

"I didn't expect to run into anyone." She didn't bother to point out that in baggy PJ bottoms and no shirt he wasn't exactly overdressed either. And it was taking all of her concentration not to stare at his smooth, muscular, *magnificent* chest. "I just assumed everyone had gone to sleep."

"I'm sure everyone else has."

"Except you."

"I was working. I saw you from my bedroom window. When you went into the maze, I worried you might get lost."

She doubted that. "Actually, I was doing just fine until someone got me all confused and turned around."

His teeth flashed white in the dark as he smiled. "Most people aren't brave enough to venture in here at night."

She shrugged. "What's the worst that could happen?"

"Giant, man-eating centipedes?" he suggested, then a sly smile curled his lips. "And there's always me."

"You?"

"You barely know me. I could be dangerous."

Only to her heart.

She smiled up at him. "Somehow I doubt that."

"You never know." His hands slid up to her shoulders, caressing her through the delicate, slippery silk. "I might try to take advantage of you. There's no one here to stop me."

"What if I didn't want you to stop?" She reached up and pressed her palms against the solid warmth of his chest, felt his heart thumping under warm skin and sinew. "Who knows? I might even take advantage of *you*."

Even in the dim light she could see flames of desire flicker in his eyes. His gaze settled on her mouth, making her lips feel swollen and warm. Her heart began to beat double time and her skin felt tingly and alive. She knew instinctively that he would be an accomplished lover. Probably because she'd known so many who weren't.

You're moving too fast, her subconscious warned her. She barely knew Chris, yet already she was sure that before she returned to Morgan Isle, she would be getting to know him a lot better. Maybe it was destiny. Or fate.

"Since the minute you stepped off that plane, I've thought of little else but kissing you, Melissa," he said, so close she could feel the whisper of his breath on her cheek. And, oh, how she loved that accent. When he spoke her name it gave her warm shivers.

A proper Southern belle would tease awhile, play hard to get. But she never had been one to play by the rules.

She smiled up at him and said, "So what's stopping you?"

He caressed the side of her face with one large, warm hand while the other slipped through her hair to delicately cradle the back of her head, as though she were a precious object he worried he might damage.

He lowered his head, leaned in and brushed his lips against hers. So sweet and gentle she went weak in the knees. But she wanted *more.* Every instinct she possessed was screaming that this was right. She wanted all of him, right that second.

She slid her arms around his neck, pulled him closer, deepening the kiss. Being in Chris's arms, feeling his warm hands on her skin, his lips, soft yet firm, on her own, felt like returning home after a long, arduous journey. For the first time since she was a child she felt as though she was exactly where she was supposed to be.

A rush of relief so intense that she felt like weeping washed over her. She'd never felt so vulnerable in her life, and frankly, it scared her to death.

She flattened her palms against his chest and gently pushed, severing their connection. And he knew why instinctively.

"We're going too fast," he said.

She nodded. So much for her brave claims that she might take advantage of him. That she wasn't afraid of anything. Right now she was terrified.

"Maybe I should walk you back up to your room," he said.

"You probably should," she agreed. Another time, another night, maybe she wouldn't tell him no.

"Give me your hand," he said.

She held it out, and he laced his fingers through hers. He led her through the maze and had them out in a few short minutes. They walked together in silence through the castle to her bedroom door.

She opened it, and turned to look at him. "I feel as though I should apologize for the way I acted out there. I'm usually not so forward."

He gave her hand a gentle squeeze. "I should be the one apologizing. I didn't mean to rush things. It's just that when I see something good, I go after it."

So did she. Maybe the problem was that Chris was too good. To perfect to be true.

But wouldn't it be nice if he was everything he seemed to be?

Despite the late night, Chris woke before dawn and for the life of him couldn't get back to sleep. Too much on his mind. Namely Melissa. Things were progressing more quickly than he'd imagined. Than he could have possibly hoped. And he was eager to take it to the next step.

He also had the crops to think about. He'd been doing Internet research last night when he saw Melissa outside. And now that he was awake, he might as well see what else he could find.

He booted up his computer, opened his browser and returned to the site he'd bookmarked—a study of botanical diseases in organic crops—immersing himself in the text.

A while later Aaron poked his head in. "You're up early," he said.

Chris looked at the clock. "It's half past seven."

"Which is early for someone who spent half the night traipsing through the gardens," Aaron said with a cocky grin.

Apparently Aaron hadn't been asleep either. Chris shot him a look. "I don't *traipse*."

"I take it things are moving right along with your princess."

"You might say that." He could see that his brother wanted details, but he wasn't going to get any. And he didn't push the issue.

"Oh, and by the way," Aaron said, "nice e-mail. You have a twisted sense of humor."

Chris didn't recall sending his brother anything lately, much less something that could be defined as twisted. "What e-mail?"

"The one you sent last night. I never knew you were such a poet."

Poet? "Seriously, Aaron, I haven't sent you an e-mail."

Aaron unclipped his cell phone from his belt. He punched a few buttons, then handed it to Chris. "This e-mail."

The address was definitely his. The subject was *Funny,* and the body of the e-mail read:

Eeny Meeny Miny Mo
String Prince Aaron by the toe
Light the fuse and watch him blow
Eeny Meeny Miny Mo

That was rather twisted, and it wasn't from him.

"That's my e-mail address," Chris said. "But I didn't send it."

Aaron frowned, looking perplexed. "Seriously?"

"I would tell you if I did. I've never seen it before."

"Do you think it could have been one of the girls?"

That wasn't Louisa's style, but he wouldn't put it past Anne. "Why don't you ask?"

The words were barely out of his mouth when Anne appeared at his bedroom door. She was still in her pajamas, her long hair pulled back in a ponytail and her face freshly scrubbed. In her hand she clutched a single sheet of paper. When she saw Aaron standing there, she speared daggers with her eyes.

"You're a jerk," she spat.

Aaron looked genuinely stunned. "What the hell did I do?"

She stormed over to him and shoved the paper at his chest.

He read it, his expression grim, then passed it over to Chris.

It was another e-mail with the subject *Funny,* and a similar, twisted version of a child's nursery rhyme:

Anne be nimble
Anne be quick
Anne jump over
The candlestick

Anne jumped high
But lost her foot
She burst to flames
And now she's soot

"I didn't send this," Aaron told Anne.

"Nice try," she snapped back, snatching the paper from Chris and pointing to the header. "It's your e-mail address, genius."

It had indeed come from Aaron's address.

Chris and Aaron exchanged a worried glance. It was disturbing to say the least. It was one thing to receive threatening e-mails, but from their own e-mail addresses?

"I didn't send that, and Chris didn't send this." He showed her the e-mail on his phone.

As she read it, the anger slipped from her face. "What the heck is going on?"

"I'm not sure, but odds are pretty good I got one, too." Chris opened his e-mail program. Sure enough, there was a message with the same subject, *Funny,* and it was sent from Louisa. But the contents were anything but humorous.

Star light, star bright
Crown Prince Christian will ignite
I wish I may, I wish I might
Watch him burst in flames tonight

"Somehow I doubt Louisa sent this," he said, gesturing to his monitor. Aaron and Anne crowded behind his desk to read it.

Aaron raked a hand through his hair. "Is it just me, or is there a theme here?"

"What the bloody hell is going on?" Anne said.

Chris shook his head. "I don't know. But we need to talk to Louisa and see if she got one, too."

"Is she up yet?" Aaron asked.

"If not," Anne said, already heading for the door, "we'll wake her."

Five

Louisa opened her bedroom door, sleepy-eyed and rumpled in pajamas better suited an adolescent than a grown woman, looking surprised to see all of her siblings standing there.

"Have you checked your e-mail this morning?" Anne asked her.

She yawned and rubbed her eyes. "I just woke up. Why?"

"You need to check it," Chris said.

Louisa frowned. "Right now?"

"Yes," Anne shot back. "Right now."

"Fine, you don't have to get snippy." She opened the door so they could all pile into her room, which was still decorated in the pale pink and ruffles of her youth. Typical Louisa. Always a girly girl.

She walked over to her desk and booted up her computer. "Is there anything in particular I should be looking for?"

"An e-mail from one of us," Aaron told her.

"Which one?"

"Probably Anne," Chris said, figuring that everyone else had already been accounted for.

"You're not sure?"

Anne's patience seemed to be wearing thin. "Bloody hell, Louisa. Would you just look for the damned e-mail?"

"My, someone woke up cranky this morning," Louisa mumbled as she opened the program and scrolled through her e-mails. "Here's one from Anne."

"What's the subject?" Aaron asked.

"Funny."

Aaron turned to Chris. "That's it."

Louisa looked up at them. "Should I read it?"

"Please," Chris said. "Out loud, if you wouldn't mind."

Louisa shrugged and double clicked. "It says: I love you, a bushel and a peck. A bushel and a peck, and a noose around your neck." She paused and frowned before continuing. "With a noose around your neck, you will drop into a heap. You'll drop into a heap and forever you will sleep." She looked over at her twin. "Real nice, Anne."

"I didn't send it," Anne said, casting a worried look to Chris and Aaron. "Hanged or burned alive? These are our choices?"

Louisa looked back and forth between the three of them. "Does someone want to tell me what's going on?"

Anne handed her the printout of the e-mail she'd received, and told her about their brothers' similar rhymes.

Louisa shuddered and hugged herself. "That's creepy."

"Maybe it's just a prank," Anne offered.

"But they were sent from our own e-mail addresses," Aaron reminded her. "Personal addresses that few people outside of the family even know. That would be an awfully elaborate prank."

"Should we tell Father?" Louisa asked.

Chris shook his head. "No. At least, not yet. He doesn't need the extra stress."

"He looked tired at supper last night," Anne said. "And he hardly ate a thing. He looks as though he's losing weight."

Chris had noticed that, too. All the more reason not to say anything. He glanced at his watch and saw that it was almost eight. "I think we should take this to the head of security. Aaron, can I trust you to talk to him? I have a breakfast date with our guest. I don't want to give the impression anything is amiss."

Meaning she couldn't spend too much time with the king or she might notice his failing health, and he couldn't take her near the east fields or she might notice the diseased crops, and he certainly couldn't mention the e-mails.

At this rate, they would run out of things to do and say before the first week was up.

"God forbid she believe things are anything but

blissfully perfect," Anne said with a snicker. "Pretty ironic, don't you think, considering the mess that she came from?"

Aaron shot her a look, then turned to Chris. "I'll see that it's done immediately. And I'm sure the first thing he'll want is to see the e-mails themselves, so we should all forward them to him."

"I bet this will turn out to be nothing," Louisa assured them in her typical optimistic way. "Probably just some harmless computer hacker trying to impress his friends."

Deep down Chris hoped she was right, but in reality he sensed a disaster coming on.

Melissa stretched out on a lounge chair on the back patio, sipping her latte, the morning sun on her face. She closed her eyes and tipped her face up, breathing in the fresh ocean air, feeling as though she could nod off. She'd slept poorly last night. She had tossed and turned for hours, filled with longing and regret. And confusion. A part of her wished desperately that she'd invited Chris into her room, while another part of her was scared to death to get too close.

Hadn't she endured enough rejection in her life?

The trick was not *letting* him get close. After all, how could he hurt her if she didn't care? The problem with that was, it had only been a day and she already liked him far too much for her own good.

She'd never understood how it happened so easily for some people. Love just seemed to fall in their laps when they weren't even looking. But despite her desperate longing for a family, the right man constantly seemed to elude her. Around about her thirtieth birthday, she'd begun to worry that she might never find Mr. Right. And now, at thirty-three, she'd nearly given up on the concept of marriage and family and resigned herself to settling for Mr. Right Now.

Maybe the trick was not to look. To just sit back and let it happen naturally. Which was tough when, as every day passed, her biological clock ticked louder.

She heard the door open behind her and turned to see Chris step out onto the patio. He wore a pair of dark slacks and a white silk dress shirt with the sleeves rolled loosely to the elbows that contrasted his deeply tanned forearms.

"I thought I might find you out here," he said, flashing her one of those heart-stopping, deliciously sexy smiles. The man was far too attractive for his own good. Or hers. She could just imagine the gorgeous children he would have with the lucky woman who eventually nabbed him. Which was inevitable. For a crown prince, marriage and children weren't a luxury. They were a duty. Like her half brother, Phillip. But he'd been smart enough to marry a woman he loved.

Not that she considered herself unlovable. But the sad truth was, when Chris did choose a wife, she would be considerably younger, with plenty of fertile, child-bearing years ahead of her. A commodity Melissa no longer possessed.

But she wasn't going to let that fact ruin her vacation.

Love was nice, but there was also a lot to be said for smoking-hot, no-strings-attached sex.

She returned his smile and said, "Good morning, Your Highness."

He lowered himself into a chair across from her, his back to the sun, folding one leg casually atop the other. "Did you sleep well?"

"Very," she lied. "And you?"

"Quite." He gazed up at the cloudless blue sky, shading his eyes from the sun with one hand. "Beautiful morning."

"Yes, it is," she agreed. "The news this morning said it should be pleasantly warm this afternoon. Around seventy-nine degrees. And no humidity."

"Some might consider that a little too hot."

"That's because they haven't lived in the deep South of the United States. Seventy-nine is downright balmy."

He grinned, and for a moment he just looked at her, a spark of amusement in his eyes.

She narrowed her eyes at him. "Why are you looking at me like that?"

"When you talk about the U.S., your Southern accent thickens."

"Does it?"

He nodded. "I like it."

And she liked that he liked it. He certainly hadn't wasted any time with the flirting this morning. A full day of this and tonight she wouldn't even think of telling him no.

"Hungry?" he asked with a smoldering grin that said he had more than breakfast on his mind.

"Famished."

"Breakfast should be ready." He rose from his seat and held out a hand to help her from the chaise. She took it and his warm fingers curled around her own. He had strong, long-fingered, graceful-looking hands. The thought of what they would feel like on other parts of her body made her shiver.

She hoped she didn't have to wait too long to find out.

Despite all the natural beauty that Thomas Isle had to offer, Chris had found that most women grew bored with the tour of the family's vast acreage and green-house facilities within the first hour. In fact, with the situation in the east fields he might have welcomed it. He should have known Melissa would be different.

She spent the morning in rapt interest, taking in the sights and sounds and information, asking a million questions, soaking up the answers much the way a parched sponge absorbs moisture. Either she was gen-uinely interested, or she was one bloody good actress. The morning didn't lack for sexual teasing and in-nuendo, either.

The pale-orange sundress she wore barely reached mid-thigh and left all but a few narrow strips of her back exposed. She obviously spent a lot of time either in the sun or the tanning bed. Her skin looked bronzed and smooth and was suspiciously lacking any bathing suit lines, and her legs were a work of art. Long and slim and shapely. About as close to perfection as he'd ever seen.

She wore her long hair down, draped in shiny waves over one shoulder. The effect was exotic and sexy, as was her accent. He liked to test himself, guessing which dialect would emerge next. In serious instances, when she was asking questions about their business or meeting their employees, she sounded more east-coast U.S. When she was excited, she sounded decidedly more Southern. Only when she was teasing, or slaying with that sharp wit, did the deep drawl come through.

If he had to choose, he would say he preferred the drawl the most. And the sassy smile that partnered with it.

At one, when he suggested they head back to the castle for lunch, she seemed genuinely disappointed to be ending the tour.

"But we didn't see the east fields yet," she said.

"They're not going anywhere," he promised. "Besides, aren't you hungry?"

"Starved, actually."

He walked her to the car, hand pressed gently to the small of her back. They had done an awful lot of touching all morning. A caress here, a soft touch there. The accidental brush of their shoulders, or her elbow against his arm. Or maybe it wasn't accidental at all.

And frankly, he couldn't wait to get her alone.

"Couldn't we see the east fields, then have lunch?" she asked.

"I could call ahead and have the cook pack us a picnic

lunch," he suggested, knowing most women ate that romantic sort of thing up.

Her eyes lit and he knew he had her.

She smiled and said, "I suppose the east fields could wait."

Using his cell phone, he rang the kitchen, arranging for a variety of fruit, crackers and cheese, caviar and a bottle of their best champagne to be prepared. After he hung up, he helped Melissa into the car.

When they were comfortably seated, she turned to him and said, "I get the feeling, Your Highness, that you're trying to soften me up."

She didn't miss a thing. He liked that about her, and at the same time it could prove to be quite an inconvenience. Although there didn't seem much point in denying it.

He grinned instead and asked, "Is it working?"

She returned the smile, but added a touch of sass. "*Ridiculously* well."

Chris knew without a doubt that it would be a very interesting afternoon.

Six

Melissa couldn't help but wonder if something was up. While the tour of the fields he did show her was thorough, she had the distinct impression that the foremen she'd been introduced to were on edge about something. They seemed wary of her questions, especially when she brought up the subject of the downfalls of growing organic, things like pests and disease. And it hadn't escaped her attention that, although the east fields were the closest to the castle and had the largest of their greenhouse facilities, they were the only ones he'd chosen to skip.

That couldn't possibly be coincidence.

There was definitely something going on, something secret, and it could be any number of things. Possibly even something illegal.

Or maybe she was letting her imagination run wild. Just because the royal family of Morgan Isle was riddled with scandal, it didn't mean the Alexander family was as well. She would just be sure to keep her eyes open and her ears perked.

When they got back to the castle, a basket packed with everything Chris had requested was waiting for them, along with a thick, soft flannel throw to sit on.

"We could walk down to the bluff and eat by the water," he suggested.

That sounded like a wonderful idea to her, and she couldn't help but think that if he really was trying to soften her up, he was doing an excellent job. "I'd love to."

"Shall we?" he asked, offering his arm.

She took it and they walked to the bluff together, choosing a pleasant spot in the shade of a knotty old oak that looked as if it had stood on the property as long as the castle. It conveniently blocked the view from the castle windows. Which could be a good or a bad thing.

He spread out the blanket and they sat across from each other. Melissa kicked off her sandals and stretched out, breathing in the salty air, feeling the breeze ruffle her hair and hearing the rush of the ocean against the rocks below. They couldn't have asked for a more beautiful afternoon for a picnic.

Chris popped the champagne—which sold for several hundred dollars a bottle—and poured them each a glass while she investigated the contents of the basket.

She found a box of gourmet crackers, a can of caviar, a variety of cheeses already sliced and a plastic container with different kinds of fresh fruit. "Everything looks wonderful."

He handed her a glass of champagne and lifted his in a toast. "To new friends," he said. "And new beginnings."

Amen to that. She clinked her glass to his and sipped, the bubbles tickling her nose. She reached for the box of crackers and he gently pushed her hand away. "Why don't you let me?"

He opened the caviar, spread a dollop on a cracker, and handed it to her, then fixed one for himself. She took a bite and the caviar exploded like little bombs of salty flavor across her tongue. She closed her eyes and savored the decadent sensation. "Delicious."

"Try a strawberry. They were picked just this morning."

He held one out to her, already hulled and cut in half, and on impulse, rather than take it with her hand, she leaned forward and took it directly into her mouth, grazing the tip of his thumb with her tongue.

The fruit was plump and juicy and sweet. She moaned and closed her eyes as another explosion of flavor overwhelmed her taste buds.

Maybe it was the atmosphere, or the company, but it was probably the tastiest thing she had ever eaten. When she opened her eyes and looked at Chris, saw the way he was watching her from under lids heavy with desire, she knew that he enjoyed her enjoying it.

"Let's do that again," he said. This time he chose a

chunk of pineapple, and as he fed it to her, she caught his finger in her mouth to lick off the juice.

"It's so sweet," she said. "You should try it."

She fished a piece out of the bowl and held it out for him. His eyes locked on hers, he leaned forward and took it from her fingers, his tongue brushing the pad of her thumb, and she went limp all over. She watched him chew, mesmerized by his mouth and his jaw and the movement of his throat as he swallowed.

He licked his lips. "Hmm, delicious."

She wanted to try that again. This time she held out a cherry. He took it with his teeth and when the juice dripped down her finger, and he took the entire thing into his mouth, sucking it clean.

Oh. My. God.

He grinned, a lazy, sexy smile, and said, "Tasty."

His lips looked so full and inviting, tinted pink from the cherry juice, that she couldn't resist leaning in for a taste. And though the kiss was meant to be a brief one, he hooked a hand behind her head, tangling his fingers through the silky locks of her hair, and pulled her closer.

She wrapped her arms around his neck, leaning into the long, lean length of his body, and a low moan rumbled in his throat. He broke the kiss and gazed down at her, eyes glazed and half-closed. "Do you have any idea what you're doing to me?"

She knew exactly what she was doing. "You like it?"

He took her hand and placed it palm down on his

chest, so she could feel the heavy *thump-thump* of his heart. "What do you think?"

She slipped her hand inside the collar of his shirt and touched his bare skin. "Then maybe we should do it some more."

He reached for her, but she pushed him backward onto the blanket instead, moving the food containers aside so she could scoot closer.

He reached up with one hand to brush her hair back from her face and tuck it behind her ear. "I thought I was supposed to be seducing you."

She leaned down, brushed her lips against his, whispered against them, "That's not my style."

His arms went around her and he pulled her down for a deep, searching kiss. He tasted sweet and salty and even more delicious than the food. She fed off his mouth, feeling as though she could eat him up. His hands were on her face and in her hair, stroking her shoulders and her back. She may have been the one seducing him, but he was definitely in on the action. When he rolled her over onto the blanket she didn't try to stop him. She opened her eyes to find him propped up on one elbow, grinning down at her.

"I'm supposed to be seducing you," she reminded him. "That's harder to do from down here."

"Sorry, love. That's not my style, either."

Well, someone was going to have to relinquish control. "I think this could be a problem."

He shrugged. "So don't think."

She was poised for another snappy comeback, but before she could get the words out he was kissing her again, and she completely forget what she'd been about to say. In fact, she forgot everything but the feel of his mouth on hers, and his hands on her body. She wished they were in the castle, in her bedroom, where their clothes wouldn't have to be in the way.

He kissed her chin, down her throat and she let her head fall back against the blanket. He kissed lower still, across her collarbone, over the swell of her cleavage, whispering sweet words, telling her she was beautiful.

They may have only been words, but he wielded them skillfully and they cut through her defenses like the lethally sharp blade of a gilded sword.

Through a haze of desire, she gradually became aware of a presence beside them. She felt something warm and damp and foul-smelling against her cheek.

Dog breath, she realized.

She opened her eyes to find a small, canine face not an inch from her own. One of those cute little yappy dogs that people like Paris Hilton carted around with them, with bulging eyes and long, ginger-colored hair tied up with a blue ribbon.

"Well, hello there," she said, and he or she let out an excited yap, which had Chris looking up from Melissa's cleavage.

He cursed under his breath and said, "Get lost, Muffin."

Such an adorable name coming from a big tough prince like him made her laugh. "You named your dog Muffin?"

"It's not my dog." He sat up and shooed the furry invader away, which only made it jump around and yap excitedly. "He's Louisa's bag of fleas."

"He's so cute!" She sat up beside Chris and held out a hand for Muffin to sniff. He sniffed daintily, then lapped at her fingers with his tiny pink tongue. "Aren't you just a sweetheart?"

From a distance, behind the tree somewhere Melissa heard Louisa call out, "Muffin! Here, boy!"

Muffin's ears perked and he let out a short yap, as if to say *"Here I am!"*

"Shoo," Chris said. "Go get her."

Muffin didn't budge.

"Over here!" Melissa called to Louisa, and Chris cursed again, but at this point an interruption seemed inevitable. She just hoped her hair wasn't too much of a mess, or her makeup smeared. Though she was sure Chris has kissed away whatever had been left of her lip gloss.

Louisa rounded the tree, looking young and fresh in white capri pants and a pink blouse. Her hair looked soft and cute pulled back in a low bun. She was graceful and petite, almost to the point of looking fragile.

When she saw the three of them there—Chris, Melissa and Muffin—she smiled. Then she pointed a finger at her dog and said sternly, "Bad boy, Muffin. You know you're not supposed to run off like that."

"He's so cute," Melissa told her.

"I hope he's not bothering you."

Melissa said "no," and Chris said "yes" simultaneously. Melissa gave his shoulder a light shove and told Louisa, "He's not bothering us at all. Is he a shih tzu?"

"Purebred." Louisa said proudly, scooping him up and tucking him into the crook of her arm. "He probably smelled the food. He's a little eating machine. I swear, he's part pig."

"Would you like to join us?" Melissa asked, in part to be polite, but also because they had hardly eaten a thing and she hated to see all of that food go to waste.

Louisa opened her mouth to answer but Chris interrupted her. "Actually, we were just getting ready to pack up. Melissa was just saying how tired she is from her trip yesterday, and that she'd like to take a nap. I was going to walk her back to her room."

Oh, yes, that fifteen-minute plane ride from Morgan Isle was absolutely *exhausting*. Although she was pretty sure that *napping* was the last thing he had on his mind.

"The nap can wait," she said.

"No," Chris insisted, spearing her with a sharp look. "I don't think it can. We wouldn't want you to get too tired."

"That's okay," Louisa said. "Muffin and I are going to take a walk." She smiled brightly and told Melissa, "Have a good rest."

Either she hadn't recognized the innuendo in the nap scenario, or she was just polite enough not to let on. Either way, she waved good-bye and walked off with Muffin trailing obediently while Melissa and Chris gathered the leftover food and packed it back into the basket.

"A nap, huh?" she said.

He grinned. "Yeah. You look *exhausted.*"

"She's very sweet, isn't she?" Melissa asked. "Louisa, I mean."

"Yes." His brow tucked into a frown. "Far too sweet for her own good."

"I get the impression she's a bit…naive."

"More than a bit." He closed the basket, then rose to his feet and shook out the blanket. "I fear someday someone will take advantage of that. And I think we've only perpetuated the problem by sheltering her."

"She may be tougher than you think."

"I hope so." He folded the blanket, grabbed the basket, then held out an arm for her to take, flashing one of those sizzling smiles. "Shall I walk you back for that nap?"

She wrapped her arm tightly through his and pressed herself against his side, smiling up at him. "The sooner the better."

She doubted it would be restful, but it would probably be the most pleasurable *nap* she'd ever taken.

Chris dropped the basket in the kitchen on the way in and led Melissa upstairs to her room. The halls were blissfully silent, and thankfully they didn't run into anyone on the way up. Not that it would have stopped Chris from going into her room. He'd have fabricated some reason they needed to be alone.

If Louisa hadn't interrupted them, he might have made love to Melissa right there on the blanket under the tree, the consequences be damned. Everything about her was so sweet and soft and sexy. He might not have been able to stop himself. He was pretty sure she wouldn't have put up much resistance, it was obvious she wanted him as much as he wanted her.

They were mere steps from her door, and Chris was already plotting just how he would get her out of her clothes, when a bodyguard named Flynn caught up with them.

"Sorry to interrupt, sire," he said, bowing his head to both Chris and Melissa. "Prince Aaron is looking for you."

Yeah, well, Prince Aaron was going to have to wait. "Tell him that I'll speak with him later."

"He said it's urgent," Flynn insisted. "Regarding the matter this morning, with the e-mail."

"Right!" Chris said, before the man said too much and piqued Melissa's curiosity. Aaron had obviously discovered something important. "Where is he?"

"The tech office, your highness."

"Fine, tell him I'll be right down." When he was gone, Chris turned to Melissa. "I'm sorry. I need to take care of this."

"Trouble getting your e-mail?" she teased.

If only it were that simple. "A security issue," he said, not wanting to give any more than that away.

"It's all right. I actually am a little tired. Maybe I'll lie down for a while." She grinned. "Reserve my strength for later."

"I'll try to make it quick."

She rose up on her toes and pressed a lingering kiss

to the corner of his lips, and it took everything in him not to say *to hell with it* and back her into her room. But he didn't want to feel rushed. When he made love to Melissa, he was going to take his time. With this security thing hanging over his head, he would be distracted.

"You know where to find me," she said, then she slipped into her room and closed the door.

Bloody hell. He lingered another second, tempted to follow her in, then he forced himself to turn and head down to the tech office, hoping Aaron had answers and they could wrap this up quickly. But the instant he stepped inside and saw the look of concern on Aaron's face, he knew this was going to take a while.

Seven

Chris stepped into the tech office and closed the door. "I'm guessing the news isn't good."

"Good guess," Aaron said.

The systems administrator, Dennis Attenborough—though everyone called him by his hacker name, Datt—gazed grimly at his computer screen. "This guy knows what he's doing."

"Guy?" Chris asked.

Datt shrugged. "Guy, girl, whatever."

"So we don't know who it is?"

"No, but statistically, most hackers are men."

"Whoever it is," Aaron said, "they managed to hack into the e-mail system undetected."

That wasn't good. "Were any other systems breached?"

Datt shook his head. "Nothing critical."

"Can you trace the ISP?"

"As I said, he knows what he's doing. He was in and out like a ghost. Completely untraceable."

"Could it be someone on the inside?"

"It's possible, but I doubt it."

"Could it happen again?"

"With any luck, yes."

At Chris's surprised look, Aaron told him, "Datt is setting a trap."

"How do you trap someone who sneaks in and out undetected?"

"You put out a net," Datt said.

"A net?"

"Think of it like a spiderweb," Datt told him. "If he gets back in, he'll get stuck. Although odds are he won't try it again."

"Why is that?"

"He's smart. He'll anticipate our next move."

"Meaning he'll just give up?"

"Or try to find another way in, through a different system."

Bloody fantastic. "Will he get in?"

Datt looked up at him. "No, sire, he won't."

"See that he doesn't. And if you learn anything, I want to be informed immediately."

"Of course."

With a jerk of his head, Chris gestured his brother

into the hallway. When they were alone, he said in a low voice, "We need to keep this to ourselves."

"The staff has been advised that the king should be left out of the loop. Although if he does find out, he'll be furious."

"Then we'll make sure that he doesn't. With any luck we've heard the last of this."

Somehow, Chris doubted they would get away that easy.

Melissa checked her e-mail, then fired off a quick message to Phillip, giving him a rundown on her day so far. Almost immediately a reply appeared in her inbox. It said simply:

Keep me posted.

Nice to hear from you, too, she thought. Though she wasn't the least bit surprised.

There was another e-mail, one from Chris that she had received early that morning. That was sweet, she thought. It read:

Meet me in the maze.
Midnight.

She smiled, and wondered exactly what he had in mind. If he would let her find her own way through this time, or send her on another wild-goose chase. Or it was possible he had other plans for her that didn't involve the maze at all?

She replied, I'll be there.

She hit Send, then shut down her computer.

She stretched out on the bed and closed her eyes. She would rest for just a few minutes, then maybe take a walk in the garden until Chris had finished with his business. When she opened her eyes again, he was sitting on the edge of the bed, smiling down at her.

She sat up, hazy and disoriented. The curtains were drawn and the room dark. She couldn't tell if it was morning or night. "What time is it?"

"Seven," he said. "It's time for dinner."

"How long have you been sitting here?" She hoped she hadn't done anything embarrassing, like snore or drool on the pillow.

"Only a few minutes."

She covered a yawn with the back of her hand. "I didn't mean to sleep so long. Did you just finish your meeting?"

"Hours ago. I came by to see you, but you were sound asleep."

"You could have woken me."

He shrugged. "I figured you could use the rest."

"For our date tonight?"

"Date?"

"I answered your e-mail," she said. "I guess you didn't get it yet."

There was a flicker of emotion in his eyes, something

that looked almost like apprehension, then it was gone. "You got an e-mail from me?"

He didn't remember? "Well, I assumed it was from you. Your name was on it."

"Refresh my memory. What did it say?"

"'Meet me at the maze. Midnight.'"

He nodded slowly. "Oh, yes, right."

How could he not remember? It was only this morning. "Is something wrong?"

"This is going to sound a little strange, but would you show me?"

"The e-mail?"

He nodded.

Something was definitely not right here. "Of course."

She walked over to the desk where her laptop sat. She opened it and booted it up. Chris averted his eyes while she typed in her password, then she opened her e-mail program and scrolled down to find the message from him. "Here it is."

He leaned over her shoulder to read it, brow furrowed with concern.

"Isn't that your e-mail address?" she asked.

"Yes," he said, sounding somewhat grim. "It is."

There was only one explanation for his behavior. "You didn't send that, did you?"

He hesitated, then said, "It's complicated."

That was a non-answer if she'd ever heard one. "Does it have to do with your e-mail security issues?"

"It's just a prank. I can't say more than that. Rest assured, there's no reason to be concerned."

If that was true, why did *he* look so concerned?

"Seems weird that whoever sent it would choose the maze as a meeting place," she said. "It's almost as though they saw us out there last night."

She could tell by his disturbed expression that he was thinking the same thing.

"You think it's someone on the inside?" she asked.

"I really can't say."

She wondered if that meant he couldn't tell her, or he didn't know.

"Would you mind if I forwarded this to our systems administrator?" he asked.

She stepped away from the computer and gestured him over. "Knock yourself out."

He hit Forward, typed in the e-mail address, then sent it off. He turned to look at her. "I'm not sure how to word this, so I'm just going to say it. I would appreciate your discretion on this."

"As in, don't go running to my family with this?"

"Yes, that, too…" He raked a hand through his hair, cursing under his breath.

"What?"

"Please don't say anything to my parents. Specifically, the king."

"He doesn't know?"

He shook his head. "As I said, it's complicated."

"Is it his health?"

Her question seemed to surprise him, and she could see she'd hit a nerve. "What do you mean?"

"I'm a fairly intelligent woman, Chris. I'd have to be daft or blind not to notice the way everyone pampers him. The logical explanation would be that he's in poor health."

He didn't seem to know how to answer that.

"You'll have to forgive me," she said. "I have a tendency to let my mouth run away from me."

He seemed to choose his next words very carefully. "It's just that it's a…*sensitive* issue."

Heaven knew, her family had its share of sensitive issues, too. "I haven't said anything to my family, and I won't. Your secret is safe with me."

"I appreciate that."

"If you ever need someone to talk to, to vent to—"

"It's congestive heart failure," Chris said, and his honesty surprised her. It seemed to surprise him, too. Maybe he did just need someone to talk to.

"And the prognosis?" she asked.

"Not good. At the present rate he's deteriorating, six months. Maybe a year."

Oh, how terrible. No wonder they wanted to keep it a secret. "What about a transplant?"

"He has a very rare blood type. The chances of finding a match are astronomical."

She could see that he loved his father very much, and the idea of losing him hurt Chris deeply.

She rested her hand on his forearm, gave it a gentle squeeze. "I'm so sorry."

"There is one treatment that he's considering. It's still experimental. He would be hooked to a portable bypass machine. The machine would take over all function, giving his heart a chance to heal."

She'd never heard of such a procedure. "That sounds promising."

"But it carries risks."

"What kind of risks?"

"The surgery itself is risky because his heart is so weak, and after the pump is in he would be prone to blood clots and strokes."

"How long would he be on the pump?"

He shrugged. "Six months. A year. The doctors don't know. They can't even say if the treatment will be effective. It depends on the patient, and the degree of damage."

"Your poor mother," Melissa said. "This must be awful for her."

"It's not something we talk about outside the family," he said. "I shouldn't have even said anything to you."

But the fact that he had made her feel even closer to him. "I won't say a word to anyone. I promise."

He laid his hand over hers. "Thank you, Melissa. For listening."

On impulse, she leaned forward and brushed her lips against his. His were soft and warm. His hand slipped behind her neck, drawing her in closer. His tongue teased the seam of her lips and they parted. The kiss was deep and searching and loaded with emotion.

Deep down she was a hopeless romantic, which had

earned her a good share of bumps and bruises in her life. Mostly to her heart, but more than a few to her pride as well. She had learned to be tough. But Chris seemed to be pushing all the right buttons, knocking down all of her carefully constructed defenses. Whether he meant to or not.

She wanted him. The way she had never wanted anyone in her life.

"This is going to sound a little crazy," she said. "But despite the fact that it's barely been a day, I feel as though I know you, Chris."

"Strange, isn't it?" His eyes searched her face. She couldn't help but wonder what he was looking for. If he saw something the others hadn't. Something special.

She reached up and touched his cheek, felt the hint of evening stubble under her fingertips. "What do you think it means?"

"I'm not sure," he said. "But I'd like to find out."

Chris sat beside Melissa during dinner, listening to her chat with his family. If they knew what he'd done, they would be furious with him. He and his siblings had made a pact, a promise to their parents and each other to keep the king's condition a closely guarded secret. Great pains had been taken with his doctors to keep his medical records restricted.

He wasn't one to confide in family or friends, but finally admitting the truth to someone outside the family seemed to take a bit of the pressure off. And as promised, she didn't say a thing about the king's health or the e-mail situation, nor did she give even a hint that she knew anything was amiss. He could only hope that she would keep it from her family as well, as it could jeopardize a potential alliance.

If she felt wary of the consequences, she hadn't let it show. Perhaps she wasn't familiar enough with the way the monarchy worked to recognize the potential complications the king's death could generate. Or maybe she just didn't care. It was possible that she believed the potential benefits would outweigh the disadvantages. And after all, when his father died, or was no longer physically capable of performing his duties, Chris would be crowned king, and if they were married, Melissa would be queen. That had to hold a certain appeal.

Whatever her motivation, she seemed willing to give this partnership consideration. He just needed a bit more time to make sure this was right before he made his move and formally asked for her hand. He needed to be sure that they were sexually compatible. If he was going to be forced to marry, then damn it, he was going to marry someone who could please him in the bedroom.

After dinner, the king retired to his quarters and Melissa and the queen went for a walk in the garden. Chris gestured his siblings into the study for an impromptu meeting regarding the latest developments with the e-mails. They fixed themselves drinks at the bar then took seats by the ceiling-high windows across the room. The last threads of evening sun shone in warm, golden-orange shafts across the oriental rug.

"Aaron showed you Datt's report?" he asked his sisters, and they both nodded. "Well, something else has happened, something involving our guest."

They listened grimly as he told them about the e-mail Melissa had received, and how the sender mentioned the maze.

Aaron and Anne wore identical frowns. Louisa looked downright scared. "Was someone watching you?" she asked.

"It could just be coincidence they chose the maze," Chris told her, but she didn't look reassured, and he didn't blame her. "I'd like to have security stake it out tonight, just in case. I forwarded the e-mail to Datt."

"She didn't find that at all suspicious?" Anne asked.

"She figured out that I hadn't sent it. And of course she was curious as to what was going on."

"What did you tell her?" Aaron asked.

"That it was a prank, and there was no reason to be concerned."

But it was clear that his siblings believed there was a damned good reason, and Chris agreed. He planned to talk to Randall Jenkins, the head of security, just as soon as he was finished here. He planned to have them keep a close eye on Melissa, just in case. They certainly couldn't risk something happening to her while she was in their care.

"Did she believe you?" Anne asked.

"She seemed to. I asked her not to mention it around our parents, or to her family. She promised not to."

"Can we trust her?"

Chris shrugged. "We don't really have a choice."

Louisa drew her knees up and hugged them. "I don't like this. Maybe we should tell Father."

"No," Chris said. "Not until we absolutely have to."

With any luck, Datt would get to the bottom of this and they could solve the problem without the king ever being the wiser.

Eight

Melissa walked arm in arm with the queen along the slate path through the gardens. She had been concerned, after the horror stories she'd been told about the queen of Morgan Isle, that Queen Maria might have the same cold and dreadful disposition. Instead she was warm and friendly and surprisingly down-to-earth. She was smaller than Melissa by several inches and very petite. Her hair was always perfectly in place, her makeup flawless and her clothes immaculate. If Melissa had to chose one word to describe her, it would probably be *classy*.

They slowly strolled along, chatting about their two countries, and what it had been like for Melissa growing up in the U.S. Did she miss it, or was she happy to be home on Morgan Isle? Melissa didn't see any point in sugarcoating the truth.

"It's been an adjustment," she admitted. "My family means well, but the last few months, I feel as though I've been in a sort of limbo."

"You feel out of place?"

She nodded. "I supposed I can't blame them for feeling wary of me."

"Well, we've very much enjoyed having you here as our guest," the queen told her, sounding as though she genuinely meant it. What reason did she have to lie?

"I really like being here," Melissa said.

"You feel welcome?"

She nodded. "Oh, yes, very."

"It seems that you and Chris are getting along rather well."

That was something of an understatement.

"He's an excellent host," she said. *And an above-average kisser.*

"You know, I've never seen Chris look at a woman the way he looks at you." She smiled, an undeniable hint of mischief in her eyes. "There's something there, I think."

Her words warmed Melissa from the inside out and she felt her cheeks flush. It was good to know that she approved.

She flashed Melissa a conspiratorial smile. "I can see that you think so, too."

"He's an intriguing man."

"He's a lot like his father," she said. "The strong,

silent type. And he does have something of a stubborn streak. All the Alexander men do."

"I think all *men* do," Melissa said.

"Chris is very loyal. His family means everything to him. He'll be a good husband and father some day. And a strong leader."

"I don't doubt that he would be." If the queen thought she had to sell Chris to Melissa, she couldn't be farther off the mark. She could already feel herself falling hard and fast.

The queen smiled and patted Melissa's hand. "I'm so glad you feel that way."

"How long have you and the king been married?"

"It will be thirty-seven years this Christmas," she said, but the smile she wore didn't quite reach her eyes. She was probably thinking of how little time they might have left with each other.

Melissa wished she could talk to her about the king's condition, tell her how terribly sorry she was, but she'd promised not to say anything. She just hoped that if he chose to try the heart pump, it would be effective.

"Life is fleeting," the queen told her, "you have to seize the moment. Live life to the fullest."

Amen to that. "That's always been my motto."

"And it's served you well?"

"So far."

"Oh, speak of the devil."

Melissa looked up and saw Chris walking down the path toward them. The pride in his mother's eyes was genuine and intense. It was clear that she truly adored all of her children.

"The king is requesting your presence," he told his mother, and though her smile didn't waver, there was worry in her eyes.

"I'll go right in." She took both of Melissa's hands and gave them a squeeze. "I'm so glad we could talk. Let's do this again."

Melissa smiled and nodded. "I'd like that."

She watched the queen hurry off, asking Chris, "Is anything wrong?"

"No more so than usual." He offered his hand and asked, "Can I walk you back to the castle, Your Highness?"

She smiled and took it, threading her fingers through his. His hand felt so big and warm and sturdy.

"What did you and my mother talk about?"

"Lots of things. You, mostly."

"I'm almost afraid to ask what she said."

"She told me how loyal you are, and what an exceptional leader you'll be. And that you'll be a good husband and father."

He winced. "Not very subtle, is she? I'm sorry if she embarrassed you, or put you on the spot."

"Actually, I thought it was kind of sweet."

"I almost forgot to mention, tomorrow I've arranged a tour of the village."

"And maybe afterward we can see the east fields?"

"I doubt there will be time. Another day." He looked up at the darkening sky and said, "We should get inside."

"Wouldn't you like to walk for a while? Maybe let me take another shot at the maze?"

"It's nearly dark."

"I think we already determined I'm not afraid of the dark."

"Maybe tomorrow," he said.

She wondered what the rush was. And maybe it was her imagination, but there seemed to be an unusually large number of security officers patrolling the grounds. She wondered if it might have something to do with the rogue e-mail. Maybe there was more to it than he'd led her to believe. An element of danger. Or maybe it was just a precaution.

She didn't question him as he led her inside the castle. It was barely nine-thirty and already it was quiet and dark.

"Are you ready to retire for the night?" he asked.

"Are you forgetting I took an afternoon nap? I'm wide awake."

"What would you like to do?"

"Something fun."

He flashed her a sizzling, suggestive grin. "What did you have in mind?"

"Do you play cards?"

She could see from his disappointed expression that he had something altogether different in mind. But he asked, "What sort of cards?"

"I was thinking along the lines of poker. I used to be quite the card shark back in college."

"Were you really?" he said, looking intrigued. "I'm

sure I could scrounge up cards and chips around here somewhere."

"Great. Although…"

"What?"

"Instead of chips, why don't we wager something a bit more…*interesting?*"

One brow rose a fraction higher than the other. It made him look young and mischievous. "Such as…?"

"I don't know. How about…our clothes?"

A wicked grin curled the corners of his lips. "Strip poker?"

"Have you ever played?"

"I can't say I have, but that does sound interesting."

"I have to warn you, I'm pretty good. But I'll go easy on you," she said, even though she had no intention of doing any such thing.

"I appreciate that."

"So, that's a yes?" she asked, not that she thought he would say no. Since they both knew exactly where it would lead.

He took her hand in his and asked, "Your room or mine?"

Chris found them a deck of cards, and they decided on his room to play. Unlike the full suites at the palace on Morgan Isle, Chris's room consisted of only a bedroom and full bath, but both were spacious and modern, decorated in a masculine theme of blues and grays, with a splash of red here and there, and dark cherrywood furnishings. The room was dim, lit only by a lamp beside the bed, and smelled of his aftershave. She couldn't help but think how well it suited his personality.

He shut the door and locked it, which sent a little shiver of excitement up her spine. He gestured to the king-size—or in his case, would that be prince-size?—bed. "Shall we sit?"

They sat across from each other, she by the headboard and he by the foot. His inexperience with the game showed. He kicked off his shoes before he sat. Knowing better, she left hers on, not that she thought he had a snowball's chance in hell of beating her. Hardly a night passed when she didn't play poker on her computer. It helped her relax after a long, stressful day.

It would be a nice change to play with a real person. She'd tried to get games going with her half siblings, but they were always too busy with their children or their spouses.

"How about five-card draw?" she asked. "Nothing wild."

"Sounds simple enough. Although you may need to give me a few hands to brush up on the rules."

Oh, this was going to be too easy.

She smiled sweetly and said, "Why, of course I will." She took the cards out of the pack, fished out the jokers, and shuffled. "Oh, one more thing. Rules are, we don't stop until someone loses."

"In other words, someone has to be naked."

She nodded.

He shrugged and said, "Okay."

Oh, yeah, *way* too easy.

They played a few practice hands so he could get the hang of it, and of course he lost miserably. "We could practice awhile longer," she offered, but he shook his head.

"I think I've got the gist of it," he said.

She didn't want this to go too quickly, so she suggested, "Best two out of three hands takes off one article of clothing. Fair?"

"Fine with me," he said. He obviously had no idea what he was getting himself into. Or maybe he just didn't care if he lost. Her philosophy was that if you were going to play, play to win. And she would.

She dealt the first hand, and though Chris still seemed a bit fuzzy on the rules, his defeat wasn't quite as bad this time. Three sixes to her straight. Unfortunately he lost the next hand, too. A pair of queens to her aces and tens.

"Let's have it," she said. "One item of clothing."

He sighed and peeled off one sock. He had nice-looking feet. Almost…elegant.

They started the second round. She took the first hand with a flush, but he came back strong with three kings to her measly pair of jacks. Despite that, she rounded out the match with a full house, which beat his two pair.

She gestured to his other foot. "Take it off."

"You are good," he said, peeling the other sock off.

Damn right she was. Three more rounds ought to do

it, unless he was wearing more than trousers, a shirt and underwear. She couldn't wait to see what he would take off next.

She dealt the next hand, sure that her natural straight would beat him, but he surprised her by laying down a flush.

"Flush beats a straight?" he asked.

"Barely," she said with a snort.

She shuffled and dealt again, and Chris won with three fives to her pair of eights.

"Your turn," he said with a smug grin.

"Beginner's luck," she mumbled, kicking off one sandal.

He lost the next two games in quick succession, and off came the shirt. She let her eyes wander across his chest, over his rock-hard abs. She couldn't wait to see more. Unfortunately for her, though, he creamed her the next two hands. Grumbling to herself, she toed the other sandal off and dropped it next to its mate.

"Not a gracious loser, are we?" he teased.

"The only one losing this game is you," she shot back, and he just smiled.

My turn, she thought, as she dealt the next hand. But he won that one, and the next. And she had the feeling that he wasn't quite so inexperienced as he'd led her to believe.

"I thought you said you never played poker."

"No. I said I never played *strip* poker."

"So what was that about the practice games?"

His lips turned up in a wicked smile. "They call it a bluff."

She should have known. But she hadn't lost yet.

"So, what's it going to be?" he said, eyes on her dress.

There was no way she was going to sit there in her underwear, so she unhooked her bra and wriggled out of it through the armholes of her dress.

"That's cheating," he said.

"We never said what order we had to take them off." And now they were tied up. Two articles of clothing left each.

He smiled and said, "Just deal the cards."

"Why don't you deal?" she said, handing the cards to him. Maybe it would change her luck.

He shuffled and dealt with the skill and finesse of a man who knew his way around a deck of cards. She had the distinct feeling she was in trouble. And sure enough, he won the next two hands.

He leaned back on his elbows to watch her. "Whenever you're ready."

She had only two choices. The dress or the panties. If she took off the dress, it would be pretty much over. Her skimpy thong barely covered the essentials. But if she took off the panties first, and then beat him the next two rounds, she would be the winner.

She got up on her knees, reached up her dress and slid the thong down her legs. Chris watched.

"I still say that's cheating," he said.

"Sue me."

He just looked amused. "My, don't we get lippy when we lose?"

"I'm not going to lose."

His confidence didn't waver, and there was a gleam of pure mischief in his eyes. "We'll see."

Melissa sat back down on the comforter, legs pressed primly together. Though she was still covered from mid-thigh to neck, she'd never felt so naked in her life.

The next round was hers, and he stripped down to a pair of plaid boxers. With no trace of shame or embarrassment, not that he had anything to be ashamed or embarrassed about. His body was…perfect.

They were even now. Winner take all.

Nine

"You ready to lose?" Chris asked.

"The only one losing here is you, Your Highness." There was no way she would let him have this one. He was going down.

He dealt the cards and she got a measly pair of aces, but she drew three and ended up with a full house. He only drew one card, and she held her breath as he set his hand down. Two pair.

She punched her fist in the air. "Yes!"

"That was luck," he said.

He dealt again, but this time he won. And looked quite pleased with himself, she couldn't help but notice.

"This is it," he said. He dealt the cards and when she picked hers up, her stomach plummeted. A pair of tens, which wasn't much, or four to a queen-high straight. All she needed was a nine and there was no way she would lose. But if she kept the tens, she could possibly draw another ten and end up with three of a kind, or even a full house. Or she could end up with a measly pair.

What the heck, she'd never been one to play it safe. Besides, she had a good feeling about the hand.

She smiled smugly and said, "I'll take one, please."

He handed her one card and she discarded one of the tens. When she looked at the card, and saw that it was a nine, she had to bite her lip to keep from whooping out loud.

"Dealer takes two," he said, meaning that at the most he had three of a kind, which wasn't going to beat her straight. He took his cards, but his expression gave nothing away. "What have you got?"

She set her cards down on the duvet. "Queen-high straight. Read 'em and weep."

He frowned and nodded. "That's good," he said, then a slow smile crept over his face. "But not good enough."

He was just trying to psyche her out, there was no way—

He laid his cards down. "Full house, fours over deuces."

Oh, damn. He won.

Chris grinned and gestured to her dress. "Hand it over, Your Highness."

Melissa squared her shoulders, accepting her defeat with dignity, but, oh, how she hated losing. "Fine."

She rose up on her knees, reached around and tugged

at the zipper, but it got caught in the fabric on the way down. If she wasn't careful, she might damage it.

"Problem?" he asked.

"It's stuck."

"Sure it is."

"I'm serious. I can't get it undone."

He slid the cards out of the way and knee-walked across the mattress to her. "Turn around."

She showed him her back and he tugged lightly on the zipper, the tips of his fingers brushing her skin. "It really is stuck."

"I told you."

"It's caught in the fabric. Hold still." He lifted her hair and draped it over one shoulder, then gently worked the zipper until it popped loose from the fabric. He tugged it slowly down and she felt a *whoosh* of cool air against her back. He leaned forward and she felt his warm breath against her neck.

"You smell so good," he said, then he brushed his lips softly against her skin, jut below her ear, making her shiver involuntarily. "Your skin is so soft."

He pulled her hair back over, running his fingers through it, then he eased the dress off one shoulder and pressed a kiss there.

One of his big hands curled around her rib cage, just under her breast, and as turned on as she was feeling, she tensed the slightest bit.

"Something wrong?" he asked, his face close to her

ear. She shook her head. "Are you sure? You seem a little nervous."

She wanted to deny it, but the truth was, she actually did feel a little nervous. She hadn't done this in quite some time. Her last serious boyfriend—serious enough to sleep with—had been more than two years ago.

It's like riding a bike, she assured herself. And what she did forget, she was sure would come back to her.

"I thought you wanted my dress off," she said.

She couldn't see his smile, but she could feel it. He drew his hand upward, over the swell of her breast to her other shoulder. He eased that side of her dress down, kissing his way across her skin. She no longer cared that she'd lost the game. In fact, she was glad she had, because what he was doing to her felt so impossibly wonderful, she couldn't imagine it happening any other way.

He eased the dress down slowly, exposing one breast, and the instant the cool air hit her, it pulled into a tight, aching point. He cupped her breast in his hand and lightly pinched her nipple. It was so sensitive the sensation was as painful as it was pleasurable. Moisture pooled between her thighs and she felt warm and tingly all over.

He had the dress pushed down to her waist, one hand flattened against her stomach, his muscular chest pressed against her back, his skin so hot it almost burned. She arched against him, could feel how turned on he was, how long and hard. Oh, how she wanted to feel him inside of her, that very second. And at the same time, she wanted it to last forever.

She took the hand resting on her belly and moved it downward, and Chris didn't have to be asked twice. He slipped it under the dress, between her thighs, touching her so intimately that she moaned and shuddered.

"You're so wet," he mumbled against her skin, kissing his way up the side of her neck. One hand toyed with her nipple while the other played between her legs. He found the sensitive little bundle of nerves and caught it between his thumb and forefinger, pinching lightly. The sensation was so erotic she cried out. Nothing in her life had *ever* felt this good. She wanted it to last, but she was so close already, just a heartbeat away from total oblivion.

Until there was a loud and insistent rap at the bedroom door.

Chris cursed under his breath and mumbled, "You have got to be kidding me."

Christ, talk about lousy bloody timing. He could feel how close Melissa was. He didn't want to stop.

"I could ignore it," he said. He nipped the skin where her shoulder met her neck and she groaned softly.

There was another loud knock.

"No," Melissa said, her voice soft and breathy. "It might be important. Maybe your father."

She was right.

"Don't move," he said, getting up from the bed. "And for God's sake, don't get dressed. We're not done." He grabbed his robe, shoving his arms in the sleeves and belting it at the waist.

There was another loud rap.

"Hold on!" he growled. He stomped to the door and pulled it open a crack, peering out. Aaron stood on the other side.

"This better be important," he barked.

Aaron looked taken aback by his sharp tone, then a slow, knowing grin curled his mouth. "Am I disturbing something?"

"You might be. Can we make this quick?"

"I'm afraid not." He lowered his voice so he wouldn't be overheard. "There's an issue."

Damn it.

"Security?" Chris asked softly.

Aaron nodded. "You're needed directly."

Chris cursed under his breath. "Give me a few minutes to get dressed and I'll meet you down there."

He shut the door and locked it, and turned to Melissa. She was sitting on the bed waiting for him, holding the dress up to cover her breasts. Her cheeks and chest were pink with arousal and her eyes looked glassy. He was so damned tempted to climb back into bed with her and finish what he'd started, but he didn't want to rush.

When they did this, they were going to do it right.

"I'm sorry," he said. "I have to go."

She nodded. "I figured as much. Is everything okay?"

"It's nothing you need to concern yourself with," he told her. "But I don't know how long this will take."

"I should probably wait in my room, then."

He wanted to tell her no, that she could wait here, but

since he had no idea when he would be back, it was probably best she sleep in her own bed. He needed to be marginally discreet, at least until they were engaged. And even then his mother would insist she sleep in her own quarters until the wedding. She was traditional that way.

Melissa tugged her dress up over her shoulders, reaching around to pull up the zipper.

"Let me," he said.

She stood and turned her back to him. He zipped her dress and pressed one last kiss to her shoulder. She turned to him and smiled. "I had fun tonight."

"So did I." He reached up and touched her cheek.

"Maybe next time we won't be interrupted."

"I'll see to it that we're not. And promise me that you won't sneak outside to the maze again tonight."

"I promise."

Not that she would have much luck getting past the guards at every door, but he suspected that if she was determined enough, she would figure out a way. Until they knew who they were dealing with, it was just too risky.

He walked her to the door and she rose up on her toes to kiss him. A sweet, lingering kiss. "Good night, Your Highness."

"Good night, Princess."

She opened the door and slipped out.

Damn, he hated to end it like that.

He dressed in jeans and a sweatshirt and headed down to the security office, where he found his brother, both his sisters and Randall Jenkins, the head of security, gathered around a desk. They were all grimly examining a sheet of paper sealed in a plastic bag.

"What did you find?" he asked.

"He was here," Louisa said, hugging herself, her eyes wide with concern. "He was right here on the property."

"What do you mean?" Chris asked.

Aaron handed him the paper. "They found this at the entrance of the maze."

It read, in neat block lettering:

RUN, RUN, AS FAST AS YOU CAN.
YOU CAN'T CATCH ME I'M THE GINGER-
BREAD MAN.

He certainly did like his rhymes.

"At least we know what to call him now," Anne said with a snicker. "What a freak."

She looked more angry that frightened. As though she was ready to go out there and kick some Gingerbread Man butt.

Chris handed it back to Aaron and asked Jenkins, "I thought you were going to post extra security outside?"

"We did, sire."

"And he got through?"

"Like a ghost. No one saw a thing."

There was that ghost reference again. But Chris doubted there was anything supernatural about him.

"Who found this? And when?"

"Avery, sir. Around ten. He was guarding the entrance

to the maze. He heard a noise from inside. He went in to investigate. When he came out the note was on the ground. He called it in immediately, and we searched the grounds, but there was no one."

"No one breached the perimeter?"

Jenkins shook his head firmly. "The gate and fence were secure."

"So it has to be someone on the inside," Louisa said with a shudder. "An employee. Someone we *trust*."

"Or someone skilled, or crazy enough, to scale the bluff in the dark," Chris said. Honestly, he couldn't decide which would be worse. A rogue employee would probably be a lot easier to expose. The idea that someone would be determined enough to risk plummeting to his death on the jagged rocks had everyone looking concerned. For that reason the bluff wasn't heavily guarded. But maybe they'd been lax. Maybe this Gingerbread Man was as crafty a rock climber as he was a computer hacker.

"We should interview the staff," Aaron said. "Just in case. Someone may have seen something."

"What if it gets back to Father?" Anne asked.

"We'll just make sure it doesn't," Chris said, then told Jenkins, "I'd like to see a detail of the current security posts. We're going to have to make some changes."

"Yes, sire."

"Do we have to do this now?" Anne asked.

"Why don't you and Louisa go back to bed?" Aaron said. "Chris and I will take care of this."

"I want to stay," Louisa said firmly.

"You'll just be in the way," Anne said, taking her arm. "They can update us in the morning."

Louisa grudgingly let her sister lead her out of the office. Chris glanced up at the clock. It was going on midnight. It looked as though it would be a very long night. And his date with Melissa would have to wait.

Ten

Hoping his meeting would end soon, Melissa stayed up until almost 1:00 a.m., waiting to hear a knock at her door. But it must have been a long one, and eventually she drifted off to sleep.

The following morning at breakfast Chris informed her that because of the beautiful weather, instead of a trip to the village, they would be spending the morning on the golf course with his parents and sisters, have lunch at the clubhouse, then spend the remainder of the day on the royal yacht.

"I hope you play golf," Chris said.

"About as well as I play poker. And I'm an above-average swimmer."

"So you'll save me if we capsize?" Chris teased,

wearing that sexy smile. And, oh, how she wished they were spending the day alone, just the two of them. Preferably in his bedroom. But with his family around all day, they couldn't so much as hold hands without raising eyebrows. They planned for private time following dinner, but after hearing from Chris what an accomplished poker player she was—he of course left out the stripping part—Aaron and Anne challenged Melissa and Chris to a game.

Chris left the decision to her, and since she couldn't exactly say *no thanks, I'd rather sleep with your brother,* she accepted their challenge. Louisa didn't play cards, but she and Muffin hung around, cheering them on. They played well past midnight, drinking beer brewed right on the island and nibbling on pretzels until Aaron—the true card shark of the group—cleaned everyone out of their chips and was declared the winner.

"I had *so much* fun tonight," Melissa told Chris as he walked her back to her room. More fun than she'd ever had with her own siblings. They didn't do things like play cards together. They were too wrapped up in their spouses and children.

They stopped outside her bedroom door. She looked up at him, and Chris smiled down at her, gently tucking her hair back from her face, his fingers caressing her cheek. "You look tired."

"I am." Between the sun and the water and the delicious food, not to mention the excellent company, she was beat.

"I should let you get some sleep," he said. "We have an early morning and a busy day ahead of us."

"The tour of the village?" she said, and he nodded. "And the east fields?"

"If there's time."

It probably would be best if she went to bed, otherwise she might sleepwalk through the day tomorrow. "Think we can fit in some private time tomorrow?" she asked.

That sexy grin was back, and it made her legs feel like limp noodles. "I'm sure we can work something out."

She could tell that he was just as anxious for that alone time, too.

"Good night, Chris."

"Sleep well, Melissa."

She rose up on her toes to brush a kiss across his lips, when what she really wanted to do was wrap her arms around him and drag him into her room. But before she could change her mind and do just that, she stepped into her room and closed the door.

She changed into her pajamas and brushed her teeth, then booted up her computer to check her e-mail. Other than the usual spam, and a few messages from old acquaintances in the U.S.—most looking for donations or an endorsement to one charitable cause or another—there was nothing of a personal nature. Nothing from Phillip or Ethan or even Sophie. It was as though the instant she left the palace they had forgotten she existed.

But could she blame them? They had their own lives, their own families. Sophie was newly married and traveling back and forth to the States with her husband, Alex. Ethan and his wife, Lizzy, had their infant son to keep them busy. Phillip and Hannah had Fredrick, and their second baby, a girl, due soon. Even their cousin Charles, whom she had felt an immediate kinship to, had settled down and married his personal assistant, Victoria, and recently announced that they were expecting their first child.

She considered sending Phillip a quick e-mail, a brief synopsis of her conversation with the queen, then thought *why bother?* If they wanted to know what she was doing, they would just have to contact her to find out.

You're being childish and immature, her aunt's voice chastised. The way it often had when they first took Melissa in. When she'd complained about being sent off to boarding school in a country whose language she barely spoke, with snobby girls who viewed her as an outsider. Or when they shipped her away to summer camp in an unfamiliar state where she didn't know a soul and was often the brunt of jokes and pranks. Because she talked with a strange accent, and she didn't have parents or siblings like the other girls. They got letters and care packages and visits on parents' day while she got nothing.

Eventually she'd learned that that all the begging and pleading and sob stories about being lonely had no effect on her cold, heartless guardians. She learned to go where they sent her without question or complaint. If nothing else it had made her tough. And the tougher she became, the less she cared, and the more the other girls seemed to respect her. But by then she was past needing their approval, or even their friendship. She was a force to be reckoned with all by herself. Besides, the fewer people she let close, the less likely she was to be hurt.

And yes, maybe shunning her siblings was a bit childish, but shouldn't this relationship be a two-way street? Was it too much to expect that they take the time to contact her every now and then? Why should it always be her making the effort? Why did she always feel like the third, or in her case, fourth wheel?

Maybe that was what she liked about Chris. He had no ulterior motives. His affection was genuine and he seemed to accept her for exactly who she was. She'd always known that if she found her one true love, her Mr. Right, she wouldn't need anyone else.

Feeling sorry for herself, and disgusted with herself for feeling that way, Melissa crawled beneath the covers and drifted off to sleep. She woke to the low rumbling of thunder and rain tapping against the bedroom window. She sat up and peered at the clock. It was already after eight.

She got out of bed, feeling cranky and out of sorts, and walked to the window, pushing the curtains aside to look out. The sky was an endless palette of dreary gray clouds that spit a steady drizzle of cold rain. It looked cold, anyhow. The sort of chilly damp that sank straight through the skin and into the bones. It had been on a day just like this that she'd lost her parents. She would never forget when her nanny had come into her room, her eyes red and swollen, cheeks streaked with tears, and told Melissa that her parents were never coming home.

She shivered and shook away the grim memories, letting the curtain drop to block out the inclement weather, but a dark shadow still loomed over her as she crossed the room to the bath.

Determined not to let the weather bring her down, Melissa showered and dressed, taking special care with her hair and makeup. Looking her best always made her feel better.

She was on her way out to find Chris when her maid, Elise, appeared to clean the room and change the linens. She had naturally red hair and freckled skin, and though she was small and very petite, there was a toughness about her. And a charm that Melissa found quite endearing. So different from her attendants at the palace. Friendlier. Not that the palace attendants had ever been rude or hostile toward her, but her routines and personality seemed to perplex them. And maybe even intimidate them.

Elise curtsied and said in a charming Irish brogue, "Did you sleep well, my lady?"

"I did Elise, thank you. Do you know where I might find Prince Christian?"

"In the parlor, I suspect. It's where he usually takes his morning coffee."

"Well then, that's where I'll look."

She headed downstairs and found Chris just where Elise had suggested. He sat in a comfortable-looking armchair by the window, a cup of coffee beside him and a newspaper draped across his lap.

"Good morning," she said.

He looked up and when he saw her standing in the doorway, he smiled. It was the sort of good-to-see-you grin that warmed the heart.

His eyes wandered over her, taking in the long, flowing dress that accentuated her slim figure, and the hair that tumbled in dark, silky waves across her shoulders. His grin said he liked what he was seeing. "Good morning."

The dark cloud that had hovered over her since she woke up dissipated and she actually felt…happy. Leave it to him to be the one person in the world who could drag her from the depths of a foul mood. And simply by smiling.

Chris folded the paper and rose to his feet. "You look lovely, Princess."

In dark linen slacks and a cream-colored tunic, he wasn't looking too shabby either. His hair was wet, which meant he had recently showered, and that had her recalling how he had looked sitting on his bed in his boxers last night, what it had felt like to have his hands on her body. How she couldn't wait to feel them again.

Even the dreary view from the window couldn't dampen her spirits.

She flashed him a sweet Southern smile. "Why, thank you, Your Highness."

"Shall I call for breakfast?" he asked.

"Just coffee for me."

He gestured to the chair opposite his, then called the butler to bring her a cup. When he was gone, Chris said, "You'll be happy to hear that I'm yours for the day."

"No interruptions?"

"No interruptions." He leaned forward slightly. "My parents had an appointment with a doctor in London." At her worried expression he added, "Just routine tests. My sisters went with them to shop, as if their closets aren't already overflowing."

"And Aaron?"

"Out in the fields and not expected back until late this evening."

This day was getting better and better. "So, what shall we do?"

"As you've probably assumed, due to the weather, our tour of the village will have to wait." There was a devilish gleam in his eye. "We'll just have to find something to do indoors."

She could think of a thing or two that would keep them busy for a very long time. "How about a rematch?"

"Poker?" He wore a wickedly sexy smile. "Are you sure you want to? After your humiliating loss the other night?"

She answered him in her sassiest Southern drawl. "What's wrong? Are you afraid you might be beaten by a girl?"

His grin was so hot she could swear she heard him sizzle. He gestured to the door and said, "Get ready to lose, Your Highness."

* * *

They never got around to that rematch.

Chris ushered her into his room, and the instant he closed and locked the door they were in each other's arms. No question, no hesitation, as though they couldn't stand to be apart another second. And when he kissed her it was so hot she worried they might both combust.

They didn't need cards to get naked this time. They tore at each other's clothes as he walked her backward in the direction of the bed. She didn't even care when she heard the delicate fabric of her dress rip as he tugged it down to her waist. She just wanted to feel his hands on her body. His lips on her mouth and her skin.

The curtains were open, but not even the sight of that depressing drizzle could drown her good mood. The gray, overcast sky couldn't smother her happiness. After this, she would never look at rain the same way again.

Melissa tugged Chris's shirt up over his head and tossed it aside. She placed her hands on his muscular chest. His skin was smooth and warm and she could feel the steady thud of her heart beating. She leaned forward and pressed a kiss against his throat, felt him shudder.

He took her hand and placed it on the clasp of his slacks. She unfastened it and shoved them down, taking his boxers along for the trip. He eased her dress and her thong down her hips, then they were both naked. For a moment they just looked at one another, and though she had been naked with men before, never in her life had she felt so exposed.

"I want to take this slow," he said, caressing her face. "But we've been building up to this for days and I'm getting impatient."

"To hell with slow," she said, wrapping her arms around his neck and kissing him. They tumbled onto the bed, a tangle of arms and legs. Skin against skin, making so much wonderful friction. One body fitting to the other like two pieces of a puzzle.

It all moved so fast, yet not nearly fast enough. She felt as though she had been anticipating this moment her entire life, and she couldn't bear to wait a second longer.

Chris wasted no time giving her exactly what she wanted, what she *needed*. He drove himself inside her, so swift and hard, so deep that she cried out with shock and ecstasy. He teased her, making her crazy with slow, steady thrusts. Speaking sweet words of encouragement. Until she was out of her mind, it felt so wonderful. So perfect.

Somewhere in her subconscious the question of protection penetrated the fog, but it was fleeting. By then she was too busy breaking the land-speed record for the world's fastest and most intense orgasm to worry about something so trivial as an unexpected pregnancy. And just as she started to come back to herself, regain her senses, every muscle in his body flexed and locked and she could swear she felt him swell inside her, and it was so damned erotic it drove her right over the edge again.

So this was what it was supposed to feel like, she mused afterward as they lay wrapped around each other, breath fast and raspy. This was how it felt to be with that one special person. The one she was destined to be with forever. Two halves coming together to make a perfect whole. It was terrifying and wonderful at the same time. And when he lifted his head from her shoulder, gazed into her eyes, she could tell that he felt it, too.

And all she could think to say was, *"Wow."*

He grinned and said, "I couldn't have said it better myself."

She should say something else, like, *by the way, did you use a condom?* But she couldn't imagine when he would have had time. Maybe, when she hadn't stopped him, he'd just assumed that she had it covered.

Which, unfortunately, she didn't.

Chris started kissing her again. Nibbling her lips and her throat, nipping her shoulder with his teeth. And she felt herself slipping, getting all mushy and turned on. Since the damage was already done, they could probably just talk about it later. Right? No point in bringing it up now and killing the mood.

No, that would be totally irresponsible. Not to mention underhanded. If the damage wasn't done yet, it could just as easily happen the second time. He needed to know right now what he might have just gotten himself into.

"We need to talk," she said.

He lifted his head to look at her. "About what?"

"Protection."

He raised one brow. "You feel your life is in danger?"

It was such a ridiculous thing to say, and she was so nervous, a bubble of laughter worked its way up. "Not *that* kind of protection. I meant *birth control*."

"Oh. What about it?"

"You didn't use a condom."

"I guess I got a little carried away and forgot. Is that a problem?"

"It might be," she said, and Chris remained surprisingly composed. He probably wouldn't be for long. "You should know that I'm not on anything."

He nodded slowly. "And you're worried because…?"

He didn't know? Had he never had the birds-and-the-bees talk with his parents? "This may come as a shock, but unprotected sex can sometimes result in pregnancy."

He rose up on one elbow, looking more curious than concerned. "You think you could be pregnant?"

"Considering where I am in my cycle, I would say it's a possibility." In fact, she would go so far as to say that it was more of a *probability*.

His lips pulled into a frown, and she thought *here it comes, the inevitable talk of* what *if, and how we'll handle the "situation."*

Instead, he asked, "Is this your way of telling me that you don't want children?"

She was so stunned by his words it took her a second to find her voice. "No, of course not! I just…I thought…"

She didn't know what to say. This didn't make sense. Why wasn't he getting that cornered animal look? Shouldn't he be leaping out of bed, putting on his clothes, ranting about what a mistake they'd just made? Why was he still lying beside her, stroking her cheek with the backs of his fingers, gazing earnestly into her eyes?

"Are you worried what people will say?" he asked.

Apparently the fact that she very possibly could have conceived his child didn't bother him in the least.

"A—a little, I guess."

"Well then, there's only one thing we can do."

Here it comes, she thought. The big letdown. She had to force herself to ask, "What's that?"

"We'll just have to get married."

Eleven

"*Married?*" Melissa was so stunned the word came out high and squeaky, as though she had just sucked a balloon full of helium.

"Just in case," he said.

Aware that her jaw had gone slack, she snapped it shut, smacking her teeth together so hard that her skull rattled. "Just in case?"

He didn't even want to wait until they knew for sure?

He narrowed his eyes at her and said, his tone serious, "I'm moving too fast."

"No. It's not that. I'm just…" She was just what? Stunned into last Tuesday? She took a deep breath and blew it out. "You just surprised me a little."

He touched her face tenderly, his expression earnest.

"I know it's soon, and we still need time to get to know each other. But I think we both knew this was inevitable."

"Me getting pregnant?"

"Us ending up together."

Maybe she hadn't known, but she had certainly hoped. From the second she'd met Chris she'd felt there was something special there. The idea of marrying him, being a part of his wonderful family, feeling loved and accepted—it was everything she'd ever dreamed of. "You're sure?"

"Unless you don't want to marry me."

"No. I mean, *yes,* I *do* want to marry you."

"Then I think if there is a possibility you're pregnant, we should do it sooner rather than later. Don't you agree?"

Though a small part of her was the slightest bit wary, the part that kept thinking this was too good to be true, the rest of her was practically screaming at her to throw caution to the wind and accept his proposal immediately. How often did an opportunity like this arise? And what if she was pregnant? They could be a family. Her and Chris and the baby. Her own little happy family. Wasn't that what she'd always hoped for?

She grinned up at him and asked, "When?"

"I imagine we'll need at least a few weeks to make all the arrangements. My mother will want something large and extravagant."

"Will a few weeks be enough time?"

"I'm sure they can pull it together. I'll have to call your brother. Formally ask for your hand."

She wondered what her siblings would think. Would they be surprised that it happened so quickly? Would they worry she was rushing into it? Or would they be relieved to be rid of her?

"I'll have to go back to Morgan Isle to pack and arrange to have my things moved. That shouldn't take more than a few days." Some of her things were still in boxes from her move to the palace. That arrangement had always felt somewhat temporary. But this, this new life, would be a keeper.

He grinned down at her. "This is a smart match."

She might have worded it differently, more affectionately, but she couldn't argue with his logic. Sentiments of love might have been nice, but she wasn't going to push it. Maybe Chris wasn't used to talking about his feelings.

That part of their relationship would come in time.

"We'll have to stay in separate rooms until our wedding night," he said. "My mother will insist."

"But she's not here right now," Melissa said, weaving her arms around his neck.

Chris grinned. "No, she isn't."

"I think we should try that again. Only a little slower this time."

"I think we should celebrate by spending the whole day in bed," he said.

It was the second-best offer she'd had all day.

As planned, Chris and Melissa spent the entire day in bed. He even arranged for their meals to be delivered to his room and they ate picnic-style on top of the covers. She kept waiting for some invisible shoe to drop, for something to happen that would ruin everything. But the day was absolutely perfect.

She even worried that their first fantastic time making love had been some sort of fluke, or beginner's luck, but over the course of the day, and then later that night, it only got better. They slept in each other's arms, then in the morning, after they showered and ate breakfast, he made it official. He locked himself in his office and called Phillip to ask for her hand.

She paced outside the door like an expectant father awaiting the birth of his first child. And when, after a god-awful twenty minutes, he finally emerged, she asked, "Well?"

"He released you. We have his permission to marry."

She took a deep breath and blew it out, surprised to find that she was relieved. Not that she thought he would demand she come home or that she would listen if he had. He was probably happy to be rid of her. Chris didn't say either way, and she didn't ask. It didn't matter anymore.

"Did you tell him why we're in such a rush?" she asked.

"Of course not. That's no one else's business." He glanced down to her belly, then up to her face, a grin unfolding across his lips. "When will we know for sure?"

"A few weeks, I guess. I'm really not sure how soon you can tell." Although deep down she knew already that she was. She could just...*feel* it. Feel the cells dividing and growing, building a tiny little person. And though things were moving along a little faster than she would have expected, she was excited at the prospect of starting a family.

The really amazing thing was how comfortable Chris seemed in their decision to marry now. He hadn't come right out and said it, but like her, he must have fallen hard and fast. To be fair, she hadn't said it either. She had the feelings, but wasn't quite ready to drop the love bomb. When the time was right, it would happen.

Chris's parents and sisters arrived home after noon, and he gathered the entire family together to announce their engagement. Melissa was so nervous her hands were trembling. They had been so nice to her during her visit, and his mother had gone so far as to hint that Chris had feelings for her, but what if they rejected the idea of their engagement?

"I think it's wonderful," the queen said, taking both of Melissa's hands and squeezing them. The king shook Chris's hand, then gave Melissa a hug and a kiss on the cheek. They made no mention about how quickly it had all happened, almost as though they'd been expecting it. Maybe, due to the king's health, they were anxious to see their son marry. And what would be more wonderful than giving him a grandchild.

Chris's siblings were a little less enthusiastic. They weren't negative or outwardly hostile, but as they expressed their congratulations, their embraces were a little stiff and their smiles didn't quite reach their eyes. She couldn't blame them for being wary. They hardly knew her. Put in their position, she would feel the same way.

She wasn't sure what to say to them to ease their concerns, so she said nothing at all. They would see in time that her feelings for Chris were genuine. She would have to be patient.

Sophie called later that evening to congratulate her, and Melissa was surprised to find that she sounded the slightest bit wary, too.

"You're sure you want to do this?" Sophie asked her. "Three weeks is so soon. You barely know him."

"I'm sure," Melissa insisted. If not one hundred percent, then a solid ninety-nine point nine.

"Well, the prince must really be something if you fell for him that fast."

He was everything she could have ever hoped for in a husband. "He is."

"I look forward to getting to know him. Maybe you two could spend a few days of your honeymoon here."

"I'll mention it to Chris. I'll be coming back to the palace for a few days to pack my things. After all of the wedding plans are made."

"I know these past months on Morgan Isle haven't been the easiest for you," she said. "I'm happy for you, Melissa. That you found someone."

More like happy that she was no longer their problem. Their burden to bear.

"We'll plan a celebratory dinner for when you're here," Sophie said. "Just the family."

"That would be nice." She didn't doubt they would all feel very much like celebrating her permanent departure.

When she hung up with Sophie, Melissa went looking for Chris and found him in his office. He rose to his feet as she entered the room. "How are you feeling?"

"Excited. And a little overwhelmed. There's so much to do, and so little time to do it."

"I mean, how are you *feeling?*" His gaze dropped to her stomach, and she realized what he meant.

"Oh, that." She laid a hand on her belly. "I think it's too soon to feel much of anything."

"You haven't changed your mind about marrying me?"

She grinned and shook her head.

He returned her smile. "Good, then, I have something for you." He took something from his top drawer, then stepped around his desk. When she saw that what he held was a small velvet ring box, her heart leapt up into her throat. It hadn't even occurred to her that he hadn't given her an engagement ring yet.

"My mother gave this to me after we told her the news. It was my grandmother's on my mother's side. She would be honored if you wore it." He flipped the box open and inside, on a bed of crimson satin, sat a ring so gorgeous it nearly brought her to tears. In the center, set in a wide gold band, was a flawless, princess-cut diamond surrounded by a ring of smaller, shimmering sapphires.

"Oh," she breathed. "It's beautiful."

"It's not very big. If you would prefer a larger stone…"

"I don't care how big it is. This is so special. It's a

part of your family history." Now *she* was a part of their family, too.

He took it from the box and she held out her hand. He gently slid the ring onto her finger.

It was a perfect fit.

Puzzled, she asked, "How did you know the size?"

"I didn't," he said, looking just as perplexed. "I haven't had it sized yet. Your finger must be the exact same size as my grandmother's."

Well, that had to mean something, didn't it? Maybe it was karma or fate.

She moved her hand in the sunlight shining through his office window and the stones shimmered. No one had ever given her such a special, meaningful gift.

Melissa threw her arms around his neck and hugged him. "I'll cherish it."

"When you become queen, you'll wear my mother's ring," he said.

If she never wore another ring in her life but this one, she would be eternally happy. The idea that she would someday be queen of the country was difficult to grasp. She'd barely gotten used to the idea of being a princess. But as long as she was with Chris, as long as they were a family, they could be beggars for all she cared.

This was the first day of the rest of her life, and she planned to live it to the fullest.

Exhausted from the excitement, Melissa went to bed early and Chris called a meeting with his siblings.

Though everyone should have been thrilled by the news—this was what they'd wanted, wasn't it?—the mood was gloomy at best. When he asked for their thoughts, Anne wasn't shy about speaking her mind.

"I think it's terrible," she said, arms folded stubbornly across her chest.

"This was the plan," Chris reminded her. "What's best for our country."

"But if you're going to marry someone," Louisa said, "it should be someone you love."

"I don't have that luxury," Chris told her. "I have to consider what's best for the country. And you can't argue that this is an ideal situation."

"It doesn't bother you that she's only in it for the benefits?" Anne asked. "That she's essentially waiting for our parents to pass on so that she can be queen?"

"You make her sound so cold and calculating," Aaron said.

Anne shrugged. "If the shoe fits."

"Don't forget," Chris told her, "that this arrangement will be mutually beneficial. We both know what we're doing. Neither of us is in it for love."

Louisa frowned. "It still seems wrong."

Chris wasn't exactly thrilled about it either. Given the choice, he might never marry. But that had never been an option for him. And if they were going to lose their father, he only hoped he could give him a grandchild first.

"If it makes you feel any better," Chris said, "I'm

quite fond of her. I think she'll make a fine wife and a good mother."

"I noticed that she slept in your room last night," Aaron said.

Did Aaron think Chris would agree to spend the rest of his life with a woman without first making sure they were sexually compatible? They should at least have that much in common. "And your point is?"

"If Mother finds out you're sleeping with her before the wedding, she'll blow a gasket."

"Yeah," Anne agreed. "She foolishly believes we're all still pure as the driven snow. Except for Louisa, who actually is."

Louisa pinned her with an irritated look.

"Who I sleep with is not our mother's business," Chris said. "But should the need arise, we'll be very discreet."

"How much do you plan to tell her about our current situations?" Aaron asked, meaning their new pal the Gingerbread Man, and the troubles with the crops.

"As little as possible. Especially before the wedding."

"And Father's health?" Louisa asked.

Chris figured he might as well tell them the truth. "She already knows."

Anne's jaw dropped. "You *told* her!"

"She figured it out by herself. She's an intelligent woman. She was bound to notice eventually. Besides, if he decides to try the heart pump, it's going to be impossible to keep it a secret."

"For all we know that worked in our favor," Aaron said. "The sooner he dies, the sooner she'll be queen."

"Enough!" Chris barked, startling not only his siblings, but himself as well. "She is a member of this family now and I expect everyone to treat her with respect. Understand?"

He received silent nods from everyone.

Even though much of what they said was probably true, he felt this irrational urge to defend Melissa. He refused to go through life having this constantly thrown back in his face. They were just going to have to accept the situation and learn to live with it.

So was he.

Twelve

Melissa had had no idea of everything that went into planning a wedding. The queen hired a world-renowned wedding planner, who brought with her hordes of assistants, not to mention list upon list upon list of all the things they needed to accomplish in only three weeks' time.

Only a few days into the planning, while they were deciding on the flowers, Melissa felt a twinge in her abdomen. Those telltale cramps that always warned her that her period would soon start. At first she hoped it was just a fluke, or maybe something she'd eaten. But the cramps became worse, and though she willed it with all her heart not to be true, she had no choice but to accept the inevitable. A sudden and overwhelming sob began to build in the back of her throat.

What was wrong with her? She hadn't cried since she was ten years old.

Mortified at the thought of embarrassing herself in front of the queen and the planner, she rose from her seat. "Will you ladies excuse me, please?"

Her distress must have shown on her face, because the queen's brow wrinkled with concern. "Is everything all right?"

She forced a smile and whispered, "Cramps."

They both nodded sympathetically.

"I'll just go take something," Melissa said.

"Why don't you lie down for a while?" the queen suggested, as though Melissa were some fragile flower. But right now she was relieved for the excuse.

"I think I will," she said. She excused herself and walked calmly up the stairs to her room, her stomach tied in knots. Though that pain didn't even come close to the ache in her heart. She had been so sure that she was pregnant. Had wanted it *so* badly. And what would Chris say? What if he wanted to postpone the wedding?

She considered not telling him until afterward. If he snuck into her room after everyone was asleep, as he had the past few nights, she could plead a headache, or tell him out of respect for his mother she wanted to wait until the honeymoon.

When she realized that she was actually considering lying to him, she felt disgusted with herself. Lies and deception were no way to start a marriage. She had to tell him the truth. If he was angry, or didn't understand, maybe he wasn't the man she thought he was.

She called his office from her room, but his assistant told her that he was in the east fields. He seemed to be spending a lot of time there lately.

"I could call down there," she told Melissa.

"Would you, please? Tell him I need to see him right away. It's urgent."

"I'll call right away, Your Highness."

Melissa hung up the phone, and all she could do was wait nervously. But she didn't have to wait long. After only ten minutes or so there was a knock on the door, then it opened and Chris was standing there.

When he saw her sitting on the bed, he frowned. "What's wrong? My assistant said it was urgent."

She opened her mouth to tell him that nothing was wrong, but her throat closed so tight she couldn't get any air to pass through. She could hardly breathe, much less speak, and her hands were trembling.

Chris's frown deepened. He walked over to the bed and sat beside her. "Melissa, tell me what's wrong."

She pushed down the knot of fear building in her chest and forced herself to say, in a clear, strong voice, "I'm not pregnant."

Not only did Chris not look angry or upset, he actually looked relieved. "Is that it?"

She wasn't sure how to take that. Deep down had he hoped she *wasn't* pregnant?

"I thought you wanted a baby."

"I do," he said. "But when my secretary told me it was urgent, I though something was wrong. Like maybe you'd changed your mind and decided not to marry me."

"And I thought you might be upset and decide you didn't want to marry me."

"I'm disappointed, but not upset." He took her in his arms and held her, and she hugged him fiercely. Maybe this was what happened when two people who barely knew each other jumped into a marriage. They just needed time to get to know one another a little better. They had all the time in the world.

He grinned down at her and said, "We'll just have to try again. Practice makes perfect, right?"

And, oh, she did enjoy the practicing they'd been doing. She did the math and grinned. "I should be ovulating while we're on our honeymoon."

"See," he said. "That will be perfect."

He was right, it would be. They could celebrate their marriage, their new life together, by creating a new life of their own. She hugged him close, pressing her cheek to of his chest. She heard the steady thump of his heart, felt his warmth seeping through the cotton of his shirt. She never should have worried that he would be anything but sympathetic and understanding. Once again she experienced that overwhelming sense of happiness. The feeling that this was right.

Melissa was so busy for the next two weeks planning every last detail of the wedding, she barely even saw

Chris. It seemed as though whenever she had free time, he was in a meeting, or out in one of the fields. Usually the east. One of these days they were going to have to finish that tour, and take the trip into the village. She was anxious to see the country she would now call home, and meet its people.

The idea of being queen someday was still a little overwhelming and frightening, but with any luck she wouldn't have to worry about that for a very long time. She learned from Chris that the king had made the decision to try the heart pump. His surgery had been scheduled for the beginning of August, barely more than a month away. Everyone was scared, of course, but hopeful that the procedure would be a success, and his heart would begin to heal.

Melissa made something of a monumental decision of her own.

"I'm going to sell my estate in New Orleans," she told Chris during their morning coffee, the brief time they were able to spend together most days.

"But that house has been in your family for generations," he said.

"In my great-aunt's family. I may have inherited it, but it never really was mine. I always sort of felt like a guest in my own home."

"You're sure you want to do this?" he asked, and if he looked concerned, she knew he was only considering her well-being.

"I am." In fact, she felt it was something that she

needed to do. Thomas Isle was her home now. New Orleans was just another place she'd lived, and she couldn't see herself ever going back. She smiled and said, "Besides, why do I need a house in the U.S., when my home, my *family,* is here?"

"Good point," he said, returning her smile. "What about all of your things?"

"All that's left belonged to my aunt and uncle." It would only serve as a reminder of unhappier times. She wanted to leave all of that behind. Start fresh. And she knew the perfect way. "I'd like to arrange for an auction, and with your blessing, donate the proceeds to cardiac research."

"Of course you have my blessing." He reached across the table and took her hand. "I would be honored."

There was sadness in his eyes. Though he didn't speak often of the king's health, she knew it troubled him.

She gave his hand a squeeze. "The heart pump will work. He'll probably outlive us all."

"I hope you're right." He looked down at their hands clasped together, grazing her palm with his thumb. "This is…comfortable."

"Yes," she agreed. "It is."

Four days before the wedding, Melissa flew back to Morgan Isle to pack her things. Her family greeted her warmly, and she was a little stunned when Sophie and Hannah threw her a surprise wedding shower. In attendance were her half sister and sister-in-law, Charles's wife Victoria, and a few family friends that Melissa had met only briefly at the last benefit hosted by the royal family. It was small and intimate, and to her surprise, a lot of fun.

"We planned to hire a male stripper," Sophie told her, "But Phillip found out and had a fit."

Melissa shrugged. "It's the thought that counts, right?"

"Yeah, but nothing beats a pair of tight buns wiggling an inch from your face," Sophie said.

Hannah shot her a curious look. "You know, I thought I heard music coming from your suite the other night. Alex must have some hidden talents."

Sophie grinned. "Oh, you have *no* idea."

"Must run in the family," Victoria said, and everyone laughed.

It was strange, but for the first time since Melissa had arrived on Morgan Isle she felt as though she belonged. She had finally gained access to the club, the secret handshake being her engagement, she supposed. She was finally one of them.

Melissa spent the next few days sorting her things, deciding what she would bring with her and what would go into storage. The night before the wedding, Phillip called her into his office.

"Close the door behind you," he said as she stepped inside.

"Is something wrong?"

"No." He gestured to the empty chair by his desk. "Sit down. Would you like a drink?"

She was half tempted to say *do I need one?* Instead she sat and said, "No, thank you. What's on your mind?"

"I just thought we should have a talk."

"About…?"

"I want you to know you're in no way obligated to do this."

She frowned. "Do what?"

"Marry Prince Christian."

Why would he think she'd feel obligated? Sure, the marriage would bring opportunities and benefits to both their countries, but there was so much more to it than that. She loved Chris. Even though she hadn't actually told him so. She'd decided to save that for their wedding night, to make it more special. And if all went as planned, she would come home from their honeymoon pregnant.

"I *want* to marry him," she told Phillip.

He looked relieved. "I'm glad to hear that."

Early the next morning the family boarded the royal plane and flew to Thomas Isle together, where they were whisked off to the castle in a motorcade of shiny black Bentleys decorated for the occasion. Outside the gates of the castle a crowd of villagers waited, cheering as they drove past.

It was a monumental day for their country, and for Morgan Isle as well. It was the first time in centuries that the two monarchies had come together under optimistic circumstances. And how much more optimistic could you get than two families uniting?

In the four days since she'd left, the castle grounds had been transformed to host the nuptials. Everywhere Melissa looked she saw curled ribbons and flowers. The ceremony would take place on the bluff overlooking the ocean, and the reception would follow directly after, held under a city of white tents on the castle grounds.

An outdoor wedding always held the risk of rain, but she couldn't have asked for a more beautiful day. Sunny, warm and dry, and not a cloud in the sky. Even the wind cooperated, and there wasn't more than a gentle breeze, even by the bluff.

There were so many people there—hundreds of guests, all focused on her—but as Phillip walked her down the aisle, the only one she saw was Chris. He stood waiting for her in his white, formal royal dress uniform. She wore the dress that her mother and grand-mother had both worn, a timeless creation of the finest silk and lace and priceless pearls.

If she'd had any doubts at all, they were erased when he took her hands and smiled down at her. After they exchanged vows and rings and were presented to the guests as husband and wife, everyone cheered.

The reception that followed was such a blur of new faces and conversation, Melissa felt dizzy. It seemed that everyone wanted to meet the future queen. She was so swamped she didn't even have time to eat, though everyone she spoke to told her the food was delicious. And through it all, Chris stayed close by her side.

Precisely at dusk, she and Chris had their first dance

as husband and wife, then Chris danced with his mother and Melissa with her father-in-law. The first man who would be any kind of father at all to her since she was ten years old.

He twirled her confidently across the dance floor, but underneath the smile he wore for the cameras and the guests, he looked exhausted.

"Maybe you should rest for a while," she told him. He'd been on his feet all day.

"They told you about my heart," he said.

She nodded, hoping he wouldn't be angry.

He just shrugged. "I suppose everyone will know soon enough. There will be no hiding it when I'm carting around a heart pump, will there?"

"Maybe we should sit down. Rest for a minute."

"I'm fine," he insisted. "It isn't every day a man's oldest son gets married."

"Yes, but you shouldn't push yourself."

"You'll be a good wife to my son." He winked and smiled. "You sound just like his mother."

She hoped she would be a good wife. It wasn't as though she had any experience. Good or bad. She was flying blind on this one.

"I want you to know how much this means to us," he said. "This marriage. What it will do for our countries."

Why did everyone seem to think that she was doing this for the country? Did no one believe that she was marrying Chris because she wanted to? Because he wanted to marry her?

She couldn't think of what to say, so she didn't say anything at all.

A short time later she and Chris said good-bye to their guests and family so they could change and catch a plane to Paris, where they would spend the first week of their honeymoon. It took three maids twenty minutes to get her unfastened and out of her dress. It would be the last time she used this room. While they were gone on their honeymoon, her things would be moved to Chris's room. No more sneaking around and worrying the queen might catch them being naughty. Although the thrill of it had been fun for a while. But it would be nice, even something of a relief, to finally settle into their life together.

She had just changed into the suit she would wear for the trip when Chris knocked on her door. Probably to warn her that they were running late.

She opened the door and the instant she saw his pale skin and shell-shocked look, her heart filled with dread. "What happened?"

"It's my father," he said grimly. "Something is wrong."

Thirteen

The doctor emerged from the king's room in the royal family's private wing at the hospital looking grim, and Chris steeled himself for the worst.

"It was a mild heart attack," he told them. "But there was damage."

The queen's face went ashen and Louisa began crying quietly. Melissa gave Chris's hand a gentle squeeze.

Chris couldn't help but feel that this was his fault. That the excitement the last few weeks was the catalyst for the attack. "Maybe if we'd postponed the wedding—"

"Don't even talk like that," Aaron said. "He wanted this wedding."

"He's right," Anne said. "It's been ages since I've seen him so happy."

"What do we do now?" his mother asked the doctor.

"The heart pump is going to have to go in as soon as possible."

"How soon?" Anne asked.

"As soon as the surgeon can fly in and prepare."

Chris frowned. "I though they would do the surgery in England."

"He's too weak to be moved. But don't worry, we have everything he needs right here."

"How is he now?" his mother asked.

"In surprisingly good spirits. But then, he's always been a resilient man."

"Can we see him?" Chris asked.

"Of course. Just remember that he does need his rest. I'll let you know the minute the surgery is scheduled."

After he was gone, Chris turned to his mother. "I'd like to go in alone for a minute."

She nodded. Melissa let go of his hand and flashed him an understanding, sympathetic smile. He couldn't help but wonder what she was really thinking. Was she upset that they'd had to cancel their honeymoon, or that they were spending their wedding night in a hospital waiting room? Or did she consider herself that much closer to the crown?

It was a terrible thing to wonder about the woman he'd just vowed to spend the rest of his life with. But what had he expected from a marriage of convenience?

He entered his father's room. He looked so small and pale lying in the bed, hooked to all those machines. Before his heart had begun to fail him, even in the first few years of his illness, he had always seemed larger than life to Chris. Indestructible. Though all of his life Chris had been told the crown would one day be his, and he'd spent every day preparing for it, he had never really fathomed the idea of his father dying. Now the end seemed to hover over them like a thick black cloud.

Chris wasn't ready.

His father's eyes were closed, but when he heard the door, he opened them, smiling when he saw Chris walking toward him.

"You sure do know how to liven up a party," Chris joked.

The king smiled. "You know me, always wanting to be the center of attention."

"They tell me it worked."

He sighed, the humor gone from his eyes. "Is it too much to expect that the five hundred guests I collapsed in front of will keep this to themselves?"

He took a seat on the edge of the bed. "It's a media frenzy outside the hospital."

He nodded. "I expected as much."

"To avoid rumors, we decided it would be best to just tell everyone the truth."

"A wise decision. I can see you'll do just fine without me."

"The pump is going to work," he said, though he didn't know whom he was trying to convince, his father or himself.

James shrugged. "Statistically speaking, it could go

either way. Maybe, now that you're married and ready to take the crown, my body knew it was time. It was ready to give out."

But Chris *wasn't* ready. "Don't even talk like that."

"Don't worry. My body may be ready to give up, but I'm not. But this will mean that you'll have to assume my duties until I'm well. Work with the prime ministers of both islands on the new trade agreements."

"I'm ready to do that."

"Just don't get *too* comfortable on the throne."

He grinned. "Of course not."

"Why don't you tell everyone else to come in?" he said, his way of telling Chris that everything that needed to be said had been said.

"Of course." He rose from the bed and walked to the door, but his father called back to him.

"I meant to ask you, is Datt making any progress with those threatening e-mails, and have you learned anything new about the situation in the east fields?"

Chris was so stunned he didn't know what to say. They had been so careful to keep it quiet. Obviously someone had snitched.

His father's voice was stern as he added, "I appreciate that you're trying to protect me, son, but I'm still the one running this country. From now on I expect to be kept in the loop."

It was nearly 3:00 a.m. when Melissa, Chris, Anne, Louisa and Aaron got back to the castle. The queen had insisted on staying at the hospital with her husband. She didn't say *in case he takes a turn for the worse,* but that was probably what everyone was thinking. He wouldn't be out of the woods until the pump was in, and even then it would be touch and go.

Melissa tried not to see it as a bad omen, her father-in-law's health taking a sharp decline on her wedding night. And she immediately felt guilty for even thinking that way.

Though no one had come right out and said it, she couldn't escape the feeling that Chris's siblings had resented her presence at the hospital. Maybe they blamed the excitement of the wedding for this setback.

Or it could just be her own insecurities skewing her judgment. They were worried and upset and didn't have time to think about how they were treating their new sister-in-law. This wasn't about her, or her marriage. And she was determined to do whatever was needed, whatever she could, to make this easier for Chris and his family. Although the idea of the king dying, and her becoming queen right away, terrified her.

She and Chris changed into their pajamas and crawled into bed—the bed they would share from now on. She assumed they would go right to sleep. God knew it had been an exhausting day. But Chris reached for her, pulling her against him. Then he kissed her, slow and sweet at first, then deeper. His hands began to roam, first on top of her nightclothes, then underneath them.

"We don't have to," she told him, so he wouldn't feel obligated just because it was their wedding night.

He pulled her nightgown up over her head and tossed it to the floor, his eyes raking over her, filled with lust and longing. "I want to."

"Me, too," she admitted.

"You said you would be ovulating. At least something good could come out of this night."

She tried not to let his words sting. She knew he hadn't meant that the way it sounded, that he saw nothing good in the fact that they had just been married. Or that the only reason he wanted to make love to his new wife was to impregnate her. He was upset, and exhausted and probably not thinking clearly. He needed her understanding, not her judgment. So instead of letting it bother her, she pulled him to her and kissed him.

Since the first time they had slept together, sex had been fantastic. Better than fantastic. Hot and urgent and almost frantic in its intensity. Tonight was different. His touch was so tender, his kisses so sweet it made her want to cry.

What better way to celebrate their wedding night, to possibly create a life?

Afterward she hugged herself close to his body. She closed her eyes and breathed in the scent of his skin. In her life she'd never felt so close to a man. To *anyone*. And she knew, without a doubt, that these intense feelings she had, this need to be with him, was love. She was finally ready to say it, to put her heart on the line.

"I love you, Chris," she said, rubbing her cheek against his warm chest, expecting him to immediately return the sentiment.

He didn't say a word.

He'd probably just fallen asleep, she told herself. It had been a long and exhausting day.

She looked up at him and saw that his eyes were open, fixed at some random spot on the ceiling above them. Maybe he hadn't heard her.

She rose up on her elbow and said it again, so this time he could hear. "I love you, Chris."

"I heard you the first time," he said, and his voice, his tone, were so cold a chill passed through her.

This is not as bad as it seems, she assured herself. It was just a misunderstanding. "And you have nothing to say to me?" she asked.

"I have to say, I'm a little disappointed."

He was disappointed?

"I didn't think you would feel the need to manipulate me," he said.

Manipulate him?

Melissa sat up, clutching the covers to her chest. "Maybe they do things differently here on Thomas Isle, but where I come from, it's customary for a wife to tell her husband she loves him."

Chris sat up beside her. "There's no point in pretending we don't know exactly what kind of marriage this is going to be."

She felt sick to her stomach. With fear and confusion and dread. "What kind of marriage is it?"

"This is a business arrangement. A pact between two countries. Love was never part of the deal."

Melissa felt a pain in her chest, as though someone had driven a dagger clear through her heart. In that instant everything became painfully clear, and the perfect life she'd imagined that she and Chris would have together disintegrated before her eyes.

It all made sense. The elaborate welcome and over-the-top hospitality. All the talk of their countries *uniting,* and what a good thing she was doing marrying the prince.

She'd been set up.

When they talked about their countries joining re-sources, she'd never guessed that the commodity they'd had in mind was her. She'd been invited here not for a diplomatic visit, but so that the prince could judge her suitability. They had paraded her around like a cow at auction, then essentially bought her from the family that had never wanted her around to begin with. They had to know. She wondered if Phillip and Chris had dis-cussed it on the phone. Laughed together about the way she'd been so easily fooled.

And here she'd believed that for the first time in her life, a man really cared for her. *Wanted* her. But as usual, she was only good for her money and connections.

How could she have been so stupid? So blind to the truth? Was there something wrong with her, some defect in her personally that made people incapable of loving or caring about her?

Humiliation burned her like acid from the inside out. She wanted to run, but she had nowhere to go. No place to call home. Her home in New Orleans was on the auction block and they obviously didn't want her on Morgan Isle. And even if she did have somewhere to run to, leaving him now could strain the peace between their countries and lead to international disaster. What would that do to the king's heart?

Did she really want to be responsible for that? Her own foolishness and naïveté had gotten her into this mess. She'd been so desperate to be loved, she had seen something that wasn't there. She had done this to herself, and she was getting exactly what she deserved.

Chris switched on the lamp beside the bed, the light blinding her for a moment. It was about time she came out of the dark. When she saw the disbelief on his face, she wished he'd left it off.

"Are you trying to tell me that you had no idea?" Chris asked her.

She shrugged. "I guess the joke is on me."

The pity in his eyes nearly did her in.

"Melissa—"

She held up a hand to stop him. The last thing she wanted was him feeling sorry for her. "Please, don't say anything."

She was humiliated enough.

"It's been a long day. I think we both need to sleep,"

he said. "Things will be clearer tomorrow. We can talk about it then."

Oh, yes. Sleep was the answer. Everything would be better in the morning. Maybe she would grow a new heart, to replace the one he'd just torn to pieces.

And with any luck, this one would be made of stone.

Melissa and Chris didn't talk in the morning. Or the morning after that.

On the third morning the king had his surgery—and came through with flying colors—and the subject of their marriage, or lack of one, conveniently never came up again. Despite the fact that she felt like a phony and an outsider she stayed beside Chris at the hospital, enduring the indifference from his siblings. Apparently there was no more need for the warmth and courtesy they had shown her at first. If they even acknowledged her presence it was a good day. She wore a facade of indifference, refusing to let them see how deeply they were hurting her. She wouldn't give them the satisfaction.

Every night she and Chris crawled into bed and when he reached for her, and she was so desperate for affection, so lonely, she couldn't tell him no. And the way he made love to her, so tender and sweet, she couldn't believe it was possible that he had no feelings for her at all. She kept telling herself that in time he would learn to love her. Maybe when they had a child. She prayed every night those first few weeks that she had conceived. Then her period started, right on time, and she felt like even more of a failure. As though Mother Nature was playing a cruel trick on her.

Next month, she told herself. *It'll happen next month.* But it didn't, and not for lack of trying, either. The bedroom seemed to be the only place she saw Chris lately. With his father out of commission, he had taken over the majority of the king's duties. He was too busy to spend time with her. It was probably for the best, because even when he was there, he wasn't really *there.* She tried to talk with him, about anything, but it seemed as though he had completely shut her out.

She passed many hours with the king and queen. He only left the castle for doctor visits, so they spent most of their time taking slow walks in the garden or watching television. They were the only ones who treated her with any affection. But they had so many problems of their own, she never dared admit how unhappy Chris was making her, or the way the others had been treating her. She just kept a bright smile pasted on her face and pretended everything was okay. Besides, how long would their affection last? Would they eventually tire of her, too?

If she had a baby, at least there would be someone to love her. Someone who needed her.

After the second month and no luck, Chris suggested they talk to a fertility specialist.

"Just to be sure," he said.

To make him happy she agreed, and endured the humiliating tests, convinced all the while that there was nothing wrong. She wasn't ancient, but at thirty-three she probably wasn't quite as fertile as she'd been in her twenties. They just had to be patient and keep trying.

She was so sure that everything was fine she could hardly believe it when, on a cool and breezy fall morning, the doctor calmly informed them that Melissa had a bum ovary and the tube on her good side wasn't in the best shape, either.

"What does that mean?" Chris asked.

"Conceiving naturally could be a challenge."

Chris didn't look at her, but she knew exactly what he was thinking. Not only had he married a woman he didn't love, but she couldn't even manage to give him an heir. His family was going to have a field day with this.

"What do you suggest?" she asked the doctor, hoping there was some simple solution. Some quick surgery that would fix the problem.

"I think we should wait a few more months and see if we get lucky. If after that you're still not pregnant, we'll consider in vitro fertilization."

"How many months?" she asked.

"Let's give it six."

She didn't think she could endure the loneliness another six months. A baby was the only way she could see to make Chris love her. But what could she do? Beg the doctor to do the in vitro now? Insist?

"I'm sorry," she said, when she and Chris were alone in the car.

"It's not your fault," he told her, but she could tell he blamed her.

No matter how hard she tried to be a good wife, the woman he wanted her to be, she never seemed to measure up.

Fourteen

Melissa looked so devastated and sad that Chris wanted to take her in his arms and hold her. He knew it was what she needed, but he couldn't make himself do it. It wouldn't be fair to her. He would only be leading her on, making her believe he cared more than he actually did. That this marriage was more than a business deal.

Coming to her in bed every night, that wasn't leading her on? That was fair?

No, he kept telling himself. That was just sex. And sex, despite what a lot of people thought, had nothing to do with love. He couldn't help but wonder, if she was so unhappy, why not just leave? Why not go home to Morgan Isle?

The answer was clear.

Despite her claim to love him, she was only using him for his title, for the opportunity to be queen. She couldn't take the crown of her own country. So she would take his mother's instead. She was no different than all the other women who had used him over the years. She simply had the benefit of royal blood running through her veins.

To be fair, they were using each other.

And if that was true, why did he feel so damned guilty for making her unhappy? And why didn't she seem all that interested in his mother's title?

Despite what she believed, he didn't blame her for their fertility problems. Now that his father was stable that urgency to have a child had subsided. They wouldn't know for sure if his heart function had improved until they took him off the pump, but there had been a reduction in swelling already. The doctors were hopeful it would work.

Chris had to give Melissa credit. She'd stayed by him through it all. All those long, boring hours in the hospital, she'd never left his side. She'd endured the in-difference from his siblings, who for the most part chose to pretend she wasn't even there, and the occasional scathing remark when they decided to acknowledge her.

And why did she bother? She had no one to impress. No one to win over. She was already in, a shoo-in for the throne. Unless that wasn't really her motivation.

Lately, he just wasn't sure anymore. And those doubts had been gnawing at him.

His brother and sisters certainly weren't making it easy for her. Chris assumed that eventually they would learn to accept her, but it wasn't working out that way, and he was losing patience with them. Finally he broached the subject at one of their mandatory weekly meetings.

They had just finished discussing how the added security measures seemed to have taken care of their Gingerbread Man. Everyone started to rise from their chairs, and Chris told them, "There's one more thing I'd like to discuss. The issue with Melissa."

Everyone settled back into their seats and Anne asked, "What issue is that?"

"We've been married nearly three months now, and it's time you all began showing her a little respect."

"Respect?" Anne scoffed. "You've seen the way she sits there all high and mighty, not saying a word to anyone, thinking she's better than us."

"How do you know what she's thinking?" Chris asked.

"You can see it in her eyes."

What they never saw, what Melissa didn't allow them to see, was the hurt in her eyes when they rejected her. They didn't see the sadness she only let show when she thought no one was around. They didn't hear her crying softly in the middle of the night when she thought he was asleep.

Louisa, who never had a bad thing to say about anyone, added, "She is a little…cold."

"And when was the last time either of you said

anything to her?" Chris asked, then qualified that with, "Something that wasn't rude or sarcastic."

"It's a two-way street," Aaron said. "She doesn't talk to us either."

"And who could blame her, when she knows that all she'll receive in return is a snide remark or cold glare? Has it never occurred to any of you that she's terrified of being rejected? That her cold nature is a defense mechanism?"

Had it never occurred to him either?

"What does she have to be afraid of?" Anne said. "She has us exactly where she wants us."

"And where is that?" Chris asked.

Anne looked at him like he was dense. "She's going to be queen."

"Are you sure that's what she wants?"

"Why else would she be here?" Aaron asked.

A good question. One he'd been asking himself.

"Something happened on the night of Father's surgery," he told them. "Something I've been thinking a lot about lately. Melissa and I were sitting alone, waiting for news, and just in case he didn't make it, I was telling her what to expect. You know, the series of events that would lead to the coronation. What her duties would be as queen. I'm not sure how I expected her to react."

"How did she react?" Aaron asked.

"She looked absolutely *terrified.* She went so pale I was afraid she might faint or be sick. When Father came through the surgery I could swear she was more relieved than we were. Every time I mention her becoming queen she changes the subject, or tells me that Father will be fine. That he'll probably outlive us all."

His siblings all looked at one another, then Aaron asked, "What are you trying to say?"

Something he'd been denying for a long time now. Something even he wasn't ready to accept. "I don't think she has any interest in being queen."

"Then why did she marry you?" Anne asked.

"I think," Chris said, "that she…*loves* me."

Everyone looked at him in stunned silence.

She had never told him again after that first time, not that he blamed her when he considered the way he'd rejected her, but she'd shown it in a million little ways. She'd done everything she could to be a good wife, and he'd given her nothing in return. He honestly didn't know if he was capable of giving her what she really needed.

"You're serious?" Anne asked. "You're not just trying to guilt us into being nice to her?"

"She told me she loved me on our wedding night," he said.

"What did you do?" Aaron asked.

"I accused her of trying to manipulate me."

Anne winced. "That was brutal."

He shot her a look. "Thanks. I hadn't already figured that out."

"I feel so awful," Louisa said, tears welling in his eyes. "We were so mean to her."

"If our genius brother hadn't waited until just now

to tell us this," Anne told her, "we never would have been mean in the first place."

"You want to feel even worse?" Chris asked them. "She claimed not to know why she was invited here."

"So, what, she thought you married her because you were madly in love?" Aaron asked.

Chris shrugged. "I guess so."

Louisa slapped a hand over her mouth, looking as though she might be sick.

"Why didn't you tell us?" Anne asked.

"Because I didn't believe her. I didn't want to believe."

"Typical man," Anne scoffed.

"I screwed up," Chris said. "And now things are going to have to change."

"Of course," Aaron said, and the girls nodded in agreement.

It was a bit of a relief to finally admit the truth. Not only to his family, but to himself.

"We're flying to Morgan Isle for some hotel's grand opening tomorrow. We'll be back the following afternoon. Maybe you could all do something nice for her."

"Maybe a welcome-home party," Louisa suggested.

"We'll figure something out," Anne told him. "And maybe you should do something nice for her, too. I'd probably start with an apology."

He would have to do something.

As everyone got up and left, Chris realized, there was one obvious question no one had asked.

Did he love Melissa?

And he was glad no one had, because he didn't have a clue what he would have told them.

It was good to be back on Morgan Isle. It surprised Melissa how much she had missed it, missed being in the palace, and around people who actually acknowledged her presence. Everyone seemed genuinely happy to see her and told her how much they had missed her. At the party they treated her like family. For the first time in months she felt…*happy*. It was such a relief, she felt like clinging to them all at once and weeping. And she used to be so strong. What had happened to her? What had she let happen?

People talked to her and men asked her to dance, and for the first time in a while, it didn't sting so much that her own husband didn't love her. Perhaps the problem wasn't that she was unlovable, but that Chris was just incapable of love. Maybe he was the defective one, not her. Which she found to be both a relief and inexplicably sad. For once, instead of craving his attention, longing to be noticed, she actually felt sorry for him.

The idea of going back to Thomas Isle, back to that life, left her feeling hollow and lonely. It was at the party that she made a decision, a decision she should have made months ago. She doubted her family would be happy, and she was very sorry about that. If it caused an international disaster, so be it. She couldn't live like this another day. Another minute. She deserved better. And though she might never find it, she had to at least try.

Just making the decision made her feel a million times better. Lighter, and free, as if a heavy burden had been lifted from her shoulders.

She felt like her old self again.

As the party began to wind down, Melissa pulled Sophie aside and asked, "Can we talk? Privately?"

Sophie frowned. "Is something wrong?"

"Maybe. Sort of."

Her brow crinkling with worry, Sophie looked around the ballroom, but there was really no place for a private conversation. She took Melissa by the arm and led her to the door. "Come with me."

They walked out to the lobby, then down a corridor to the business offices. When they were inside one of the offices she closed the door, turned to Melissa and asked, "Is he hurting you?"

The question, and the ferocity with which she asked it, stunned Melissa for a second. "Hurting me?"

"I could tell from the second you arrived that something was wrong. Is he physically abusing you? Because if he is, royalty or not, I'll have to hurt him back."

"Of course not! Chris would never do that. He's a good man." *Just not so hot a husband.*

"Then what's wrong?"

She'd had no idea she was so transparent. That it was so obvious she was unhappy. Or maybe Sophie was just exceptionally perceptive.

In that case, she might as well be totally honest. "I asked to speak to you because frankly, I'm afraid of what Phillip's reaction will be. The blow might be gentler coming from you."

"What blow?"

"I'm leaving Chris."

Sophie stunned Melissa again by pulling her into her arms and hugging her. "I am so sorry. I was afraid this might happen when you rushed into this the way you did."

Melissa pulled back from her embrace. "That was the whole point, wasn't it?"

"What do you mean?"

"Look, I know it was a setup. That it was never meant to be more than a business deal. I thought I could handle it, for the good of the country and all that, but the truth is, I'm miserable."

Sophie frowned. "Back up a minute. What do you mean, about it being a setup?"

"The invitation to Thomas Isle. All the attention they showered on me to make me feel welcome. That was a nice touch, by the way."

Sophie looked hopelessly confused. "Melissa, what are you talking about?"

"Prince Christian needed a wife and I was the convenient choice. A pawn in your political game."

Sophie gaped at her. "My God, Melissa, you don't honestly think we would do that to you?"

She had, until just then. Now she had to wonder if she'd been wrong. "I figured you never really wanted me around anyway."

Sophie took her by the shoulders. "I assure you, if

there was any sort of setup, we knew *nothing* about it. As far as we knew it was just a diplomatic visit. We were *stunned* when you decided to stay and marry the prince. And why in heaven's name would you think we didn't want you around?"

"I was an outsider…a complication. You can't say it hasn't been easier with me gone."

Sophie sighed, looking inexplicably sad. "Melissa, our father left a legacy of scandal, and all we could do is pick up the pieces and move on. Was it complicated? You bet. Has it been easy? Not always. But that certainly wasn't your fault. Despite the circumstances, you're *family.* One of us. You were *always* welcome at the palace. And you always will be."

She hoped that was true. "You don't think Phillip will be angry?"

"Of course not. He'll be happy to have you home. We all will."

Melissa felt limp with relief, as though the nightmare was truly over. "It may not be a sound move diplomatically."

"Screw diplomacy. You're coming home."

Home. The idea sounded so wonderful she felt like weeping. She loved Chris, and she so desperately wanted him to love her back, but that was never going to happen. And they were both miserable.

"I'll talk to Phillip and make the arrangements," Sophie said. "We'll have your things sent here so you don't even have to go back there."

The thought of never seeing the king and queen again made her heart sting. They had been good to her, and she hated the idea of disappointing them. They were the closest thing to parents that she'd had since she lost her own mother and father. She would always appreciate that. She didn't expect them to understand what she was going to do, but she hoped some day they would forgive her.

It was well after 1:00 a.m. when they got back to the palace. As usual, when she and Chris climbed into bed, he reached for her, and for the first time she refused him.

"I'm tired," she said, turning away from him. She wondered if he would insist, or try to convince her, but after a moment of silence, he turned over and went to sleep.

If only he'd told her he loved her. That's all it would have taken. But she couldn't expect him to say something he didn't mean. That wouldn't mean anything to her.

Though it saddened her to the depths of her soul, she knew their marriage was over.

Phillip called Melissa to his office the next morning. "I talked to Sophie. She says that you want to come home."

There was that word again. *Home.* But what if, unlike Sophie, he really didn't want her there?

"Are you angry?" she asked.

"Angry?" He looked surprised by the question. "Why would I be angry?"

"I just want you to know that I don't have to stay at

the palace. I'm sure I could find a nice place in town, or even build something new."

He gestured to the sofa. "Please, have a seat."

She sat down, and he sat beside her. "Melissa, I know that my disposition is not always the warmest. A trait I inherited from our father, unfortunately. Hannah is constantly telling me that I need to lighten up. But I want you to know, and I mean this sincerely, from the bottom of my heart, that you were always, and always will be welcome to stay at the palace. It doesn't matter how or why, you're our family, and your place is with *us*."

His words, said so sincerely, touched her somewhere deep down. If only she had known that months ago, when she first came to Morgan Isle. She might not have been so vulnerable. She would have seen Chris's so-called affection for what it really was.

Not that she was blaming Phillip. This was no one's fault but her own.

"That's good to know," she said.

"I know Sophie already told you this, but I just wanted to clarify that there was never any 'arrangement.' Not of the marital kind. Although in retrospect, I see that whatever was said was misconstrued by them or us, or maybe both. And I take full responsibility."

"To be honest, I think it was all a big, stupid misunderstanding. As much my fault as theirs. It would be best if we all just let it drop."

"Have you talked to him yet?"

"Chris?" she asked and he nodded. She shook her head.

He looked at his watch. "Your plane is due to leave in less than an hour. If you're not going home with him, you should probably let him know."

"You're right."

This wasn't something she was looking forward to, but it had to be done.

Melissa found Chris in the guest suite, packing the last of his things.

"Our flight leaves in forty minutes," he said without looking at her. Maybe he was upset that she'd turned him down last night. Maybe his feelings had been hurt. It could mean that he did care.

Don't do that to yourself, Melissa. Just get this over with.

"I know it does," she said. "I won't be on it."

"You want to stay here longer?"

A lot longer. Like, forever. "Something like that."

He finally turned to her. He looked tired, as though he'd barely slept. "You're mad at me. I get it."

"Why would you think I'm mad?"

"You pretty much ignored me all last night at the party. Dancing with just about every man in the room but me."

She was surprised he noticed. "Not *every* man."

He glared at her. "You want to get on with it? Just say what you have to say, and let's go home."

He really was upset. Their first real fight as husband and wife. Their first and their last.

"I can't do this anymore, Chris."

"Do what?"

"Be with you. Stay on Thomas Isle. I'm lonely and miserable."

"I've talked to my brother and sisters," he said. "Things will be different when we get back. They'll be nice to you now."

And that was supposed to fix everything? "The only person whose actions I give a damn about are yours. The way you treat me, I feel so…*used*."

"It isn't like that," he insisted.

"That's sure how it feels to me."

"So you're just going to give up?"

"At least I *tried*. What have you contributed to this marriage?"

He didn't seem to know how to answer that, so he didn't. "So you're saying it's over?"

"It is for me. The truth is, it has been for a while."

"You're leaving me?"

"Don't worry, I'm sure there are countless women out there who would be happy to marry themselves into a royal title. Younger ones, who will have no trouble bearing lots of children for you."

His expression darkened. "Our fertility issues have nothing to do with my feelings for you."

"You mean *my* fertility issues."

"I never once blamed you."

"But you didn't *not* blame me. And I didn't feel any less like a failure." She stepped closer, feeling almost sorry for him. He probably wasn't used to being rejected. When it came right down to it, she was the stronger one. She had the courage to let go.

"Look, we gave it a shot," she said. "We should quit while we're ahead. Call it even. But this won't affect the trade agreements. I'll see to that."

He shook his head, as though searching for the right thing to say. Something that would make her change her mind, although for the life of her, she didn't know why he cared.

Finally he said, "I can't change who I am, Melissa."

He'd hit the nail right on the head.

"I know," she told him, "and that's exactly why I have to go."

Fifteen

Chris had looked forward to getting back home, getting on with his life, but as the car pulled up to the castle and he saw Aaron, Anne and Louisa waiting—probably for that warm welcome home they'd talked about—he wished he was anywhere else.

The car rolled to a stop, and when he climbed out alone, all three looked confused.

"Melissa isn't with you?" Louisa asked.

"Do you see her anywhere?" Chris snapped.

Startled, she shrank away, looking wounded.

Anne wasn't affected by his sharp tone. "Where is she, then?"

He stomped past them to the door, tossing back over his shoulder, "Morgan Isle."

"When is she coming back?" Aaron called.

He stopped abruptly and turned. He wanted to shout at them, say that if they'd only been nicer to her, this never would have happened. But the only one to blame for this mess was him. "Never," he told them. "She's never coming back."

He left them in stunned silence and went straight to his room. He didn't feel up to explaining this to his parents. He didn't even know where to begin.

The second he stepped in his room and closed the door, he knew it was a mistake. Everything here reminded him of Melissa. The trinkets and keepsakes on the dresser, and the photo of her and her parents. He could even smell her. A mix of her shampoo and soap and the citrus body spray she used. She'd left an indelible mark on everything.

He walked over to the dresser and picked up the photo. She and her parents looked so happy. She didn't talk about it much, but he knew how devastating it had been for her to lose them, then to feel so unwanted by her guardians. She'd moved to Morgan Isle, where she had admittedly never felt as though she fit in. Then they'd invited her here, where she was welcomed with open arms and affection, and the instant she became family, was treated like a trespasser. And all she'd ever wanted was someone to love her.

Talk about playing a cruel trick. And all because of a few crossed wires. Because he thought they were on the same page in regard to their arranged marriage.

It's a wonder she hadn't left him that first week. They might all have been better off.

He wanted to believe that this was for the best, but he wasn't sure what to believe. He would be lying if he said he hadn't grown fond of her. He actually liked having her around. And not just for the sex, although that was beyond satisfying. The idea of not waking up to feel her curled against him, not seeing her beautiful smile again, caused a strange aching sensation in his chest.

Maybe it he wasn't ready to let go. To give up. Maybe things could be different.

He set the photo back down. She'd asked him to have her things shipped home to her. But *this* was her home. She belonged here, with him. She had to know that. Maybe it was like poker and she was bluffing in attempt to get him to call his hand. Trying to *make* him love her.

If she really loved him, she would be back, he told himself, feeling better already. He gave her a couple of days, a week, tops, before she came crawling back to him. But all he got at the end of that week was a fat envelope from her attorney filled with divorce papers. There was also a very firmly worded letter demanding he return her things to her immediately.

Not exactly the actions of a woman planning to come back.

He tossed it all directly in the trash.

In that week, the curious ache in his chest had turned into a searing pain, as though someone had driven a hot iron through him and then proceeded to yank it back and forth until he felt like his insides were leaking to the outside. Soon he would be just a shell of a man. Skin and bone with no substance.

No soul.

Melissa had taken it with her.

When a group of her henchmen flew to the island to physically fetch her things themselves, he refused to let them past the main gate.

"You obviously love her," Aaron said. "Why don't you just go get her?"

"She'll be back," he said.

He looked at Chris like he was hopeless. Everyone had been looking at him that way lately. Except his mother, who wasn't looking at or speaking to him at all. And hadn't been since he'd told her the truth about everything that had happened. He hadn't really had a choice. She'd demanded to know the truth, and when she wanted something, the word *no* wasn't part of his vocabulary.

She'd had pretty much the same reaction as his siblings. "She didn't know it was an arrangement?"

He told her the entire story, and when he was finished explaining, she looked as though she wanted to strike him. "That poor girl. I raised you better than this."

He tried to make excuses, and all he got from her was, "I want my daughter-in-law back."

He'd never seen her look so disappointed in him, which stung more than any form of corporal punishment ever could.

By the end of the second week, when he hadn't gone after Melissa and still refused to turn over her things, holding them like some warped form of ransom, his brother and sisters stopped talking to him, too.

"What the bloody hell is the matter with you?" was the last thing Anne said to him. Louisa just stood there shaking her head sadly, then said, "I'm so disappointed in you." Which coming from her was pretty harsh.

The next morning as he was in his closet dressing for work, he heard the bedroom door open. He got up and walked out, and when he realized who it was standing in his bedroom, her back to him, for an instant he was sure he was hallucinating. "Melissa?"

She spun around, clutching the photo of herself and her parents, looking as surprised to see him as he was to see her. "What are you doing here?"

Was that some sort of trick question? "Uh…I live here?"

"You're not supposed to be here," she snapped with that sharp Southern twang. Over the last few months she'd lost that, and only now did he realize how much he'd missed it. Missed *her.* It was good to hear her sounding like her old self. The one that was fun and spunky, and wasn't afraid to talk back to him, tell him what was on her mind. It pained him to know that he'd made her so miserable he'd broken her spirit.

It was a bit ironic that now he was the one feeling isolated, lonely and like a complete failure. And finally, when he thought it would never be clear, never make sense, something in his head, or maybe in his heart, finally snapped, or shifted into place. He wasn't sure exactly what happened. All he knew was that one minute he was confused as hell, unsure of what to do next, how to fix the mess he'd made, and the next he knew without a shadow of doubt that he was in love with Melissa. It seemed so damned simple he didn't know why he hadn't figured it out before.

This may have started out as a business arrangement, but something had happened to him. Slowly, gradually, being with Melissa had changed him. He used to believe that marriage was nothing more than a duty. He could take it or leave it. And maybe with any other woman as his wife, that would still be true.

Now he couldn't imagine his life without Melissa by his side. He could only hope she would give him a chance to make it up to her.

He had to tell her, convince her to come home. And the only way that was going to happen was if he swallowed his outrageously over-inflated pride, stuck his tail between his legs where it belonged, and went crawling back to her.

Though he could see she was angry as hell, he couldn't help smiling. He could hardly wait for the opportunity to gather her into his arms and just hold her. Although he feared that if he were to try now, she was likely to deck him.

"Where am I supposed to be?" he asked her.

"Away on business."

"I am?"

"Your mother called and said you would be gone, and that I should come and get my things."

His mother had said she wanted Melissa back. She must have figured that if Chris wouldn't come to his senses, she would do it for him. And damned if she hadn't been right.

"Well, as you can see, I'm here. Not away on business." He took a step toward her, and she took one back, colliding with the dresser.

She looked genuinely alarmed. "I'm just here for my things. I don't want any trouble."

"What kind of trouble were you expecting?"

Her chin rose a notch. "That kind that would necessitate the two very large bodyguards I brought with me."

He looked around the room. "I don't see any bodyguards."

She drew her lower lip between her teeth, glancing nervously past him to the door. "They're downstairs, watching the doors in case you come in and try to stop me. All I have to do is yell and they'll come running."

Even if they heard her they would never make it in time. He was between her and the door. Not to mention they were outnumbered two to a couple dozen in the castle alone.

"You would really sic your bodyguards on me?"

"If necessary."

He walked slowly backward toward the door, and her

eyes widened a little. "What is it you think I'm going to do to you?"

"If you're trying to intimidate me, it isn't going to work."

He backed the door shut, and when he snapped the lock, she flinched. "Maybe it's just me, but you sure look intimidated."

She swallowed. "I could scream."

He started walking slowly toward her. "Why would you do that?"

"I know karate," she warned him.

He knew for a fact that she didn't. "Again, I ask, what is it you think I'm going to do to you?"

"I don't know!" she said, looking exasperated. "That's the problem. Your behavior these last few weeks has been…odd."

"Odd?"

She narrowed her eyes at him. "You don't think it's just a little creepy that you refuse to give me back my things?"

He shrugged. "Maybe a little. But I had a good reason."

"What reason?"

"I wanted them here for you when you came home."

"See, that makes you sound like a stalker."

"Having my wife home makes me sound like a stalker? In what penal system?"

"This isn't my home. And as soon as you sign the divorce papers, I won't be your wife anymore."

"I tossed them in the trash."

"Why?"

"Because you love me."

She frowned and shook her head, rubbing her temples as if the whole conversation was giving her a headache. "I'm not doing this again. Please just let me get my things and go."

She started to move toward the door but he stepped in her way. "Just hear me out. Five minutes, that's all I'm asking."

Since it was obvious she had little choice in the matter, she said, "Okay, five minutes."

"The way I figure it, you don't want the man you married."

She nodded slowly, looking totally confused. "Hence the divorce papers."

"What I mean is, you want the man I was before we were married. The man I was before our wedding night. That's the man you love. Right?"

She looked suddenly and inexplicably sad. "But you aren't that man."

"Yes, I am. He's always been in there. And that man loves you."

She cupped her hands over her ears and scrunched up her face as though she was in pain. "Please don't say things like that."

"You want to know the truth?"

She shook her head.

"On our wedding night, when you told me you loved me, you scared the living hell out of me. Since the day

I was born, my life has been meticulously planned out for me. And never, in all that preparation, was love ever mentioned. It was not part of that plan."

Her face was still scrunched, but she wasn't holding her hands very tightly over her ears. He walked closer until he was standing right in front of her.

"I really cared about you, Melissa. The day we were married, maybe it wasn't love yet, but I had very strong feelings for you. I trusted you. Then you said you loved me. Since that had never been part of the plan, I was sure you were only saying it to manipulate me. It wouldn't be the first time. And I honestly had believed you were different. I felt…*betrayed*."

Her hands dropped to her sides. "I would never say it if I didn't mean it."

"I know that now."

"You made me miserable."

"I know that, too. And I'm sorry. All I can do is promise that I'll never do it again. If you give me another chance."

"Why should I believe you?"

"Because I wouldn't say it if I didn't mean it."

"I knew this would happen," she said, looking up at him. "This is why I didn't want to come here."

"Why?"

"Because I knew you would start saying all of these wonderful things and then I would start to melt." The hint of a grin curled one corner of her mouth. "Then, even if I knew it was bad for me, I'd end up falling in love with you all over again. Which I have. Thanks a lot."

"Does that mean you're coming home?"

She hesitated, then bit her lip and nodded.

He smiled and held out his arms, and she stepped into them. She wrapped her arms around him, and he wrapped his around her, and they just held each other.

"I love you, Chris."

This time when she said it he didn't feel confused or betrayed. He felt like he was probably the happiest man on earth. "I love you too."

"Both?"

"The first Chris and the second Chris."

"And for the record, I loved you both."

"You did?"

"Yeah, but the first you was my friend, too, and I really missed him."

But he was here now. Exactly where he was supposed to be. And so was Melissa.

In his arms, right where she belonged.

* * * * *

Don't miss Prince Aaron's story,
Christmas with the Prince, available
November 2009 from Silhouette Desire.
And don't miss Bossman Billionaire, Mr. August's
Man of the Month from Silhouette Desire.

*Celebrate 60 years of pure
reading pleasure with Harlequin!*

To commemorate the event, Harlequin Intrigue®
is thrilled to invite you to the wedding of The Colby
Agency's J. T. Baxley and his bride, Eve Mattson.

That is, of course, if J.T. can find the woman who
left him at the altar. Considering he's a private in-
vestigator for one of the top agencies in the
country—the best of the best—that shouldn't be
a problem. The real setback is that his bride isn't
who she appears to be…and her mysterious past
has put them both in danger.

*Enjoy an exclusive glimpse of
Debra Webb's latest addition to*
**THE COLBY AGENCY: ELITE
RECONNAISSANCE DIVISION**

THE BRIDE'S SECRETS

Available August 2009 from Harlequin Intrigue®.

The dark figures on the dock were still firing. The bullets cutting through the surface of the water without the warning boom of shots told Eve they were using silencers.

That was to her benefit. Silencers decreased the accuracy of every shot and lessened the range.

She grabbed for the rocks. Scrambled through the darkness. Bumped her knee on a boulder. Cursed.

Burrowing into the waist-deep grass, she kept low and crawled forward. Faster. Pushed harder. Needed as much distance as possible.

Shots pinged on the rocks.

J.T. scrambled alongside her.

He was breathing hard.

They had to stay close to the ground until they reached the next row of warehouses. Even though she was relatively certain they were out of range at this point, she wasn't taking any risks. And she wasn't slowing down.

J.T. had to keep up.

The splat of a bullet hitting the ground next to Eve had her rolling left. Maybe they weren't completely out of range.

She bumped J.T. He grunted.

His injured arm. Dammit. She could apologize later.

Half a dozen more yards.

Almost in the clear.

As she reached the cover of the alley between the first two warehouses she tensed.

Silence.

No pings or splats.

She glanced back at the dock. Deserted.

Time to run.

Her car was parked another block down.

Pushing to her feet, she sprinted forward. The wet bag dragged at her shoulder. She ignored it.

By the time she reached the lot where her car was parked, she had dug the keys from her pocket and hit the fob. Six seconds later she was behind the wheel. She hit the ignition as J.T. collapsed into the passenger seat. Tires squealed as she spun out of the slot.

"What the hell did you do to me?"

From the corner of her eye she watched him shake his head in an attempt to clear it.

He would be pissed when she told him about the tranquilizer.

She'd needed him cooperative until she formulated a plan. A drug-induced state of unconsciousness had been the fastest and most efficient method to ensure his continued solidarity.

"I can't really talk right now." Eve weaved into the right lane as the street widened to four lanes. What she needed was traffic. It was Saturday night—shouldn't be that difficult to find as soon as they were out of the old warehouse district.

A glance in the rearview mirror warned that their unwanted company had caught up.

Sensing her tension, J.T. turned to peer over his left shoulder.

"I hope you have a plan B."

She shot him a look. "There's always plan G." Then she pulled the Glock out of her waistband.

Cutting the steering wheel left, she slid between two vehicles. Another veer to the right and she'd put several cars between hers and the enemy.

She was betting they wouldn't pull out the firepower in the open like this, but a girl could never be too sure when it came to an unknown enemy.

Deep blending was the way to go.

Two traffic lights ahead the marquis of a movie theater provided exactly the opportunity she was looking for.

The digital numbers on the dash indicated it was just

past midnight. Perfect timing. The late movie would be purging its audience into the crowd of teenagers who liked hanging out in the parking lot.

She took a hard right onto the property that sported a twelve-screen theater, numerous fast-food hot spots and a chain superstore. Speeding across the lot, she selected a lane of parking slots. Pulling in as close to the theater entrance as possible, she shut off the engine and reached for her door.

"Let's go."

Thankfully he didn't argue.

Rounding the hood of her car, she shoved the Glock into her bag, then wrapped her arm around J.T.'s and merged into the crowd.

With her free hand she finger-combed her long hair. It was soaked, as were her clothes. The kids she bumped into noticed, gave her death-ray glares.

They just didn't know.

As she and J.T. moved in closer to the building, she grabbed a baseball cap from an innocent bystander. The crowd made it easy. The kid who owned the cap had made it even easier by stuffing the cap bill-first into his waistband at the small of his back.

Pushing through the loitering crowd, she made her way to the side of the building next to the main entrance. She pushed J.T. against the wall and dropped her bag to the ground. Peeled off her tee and let it fall.

His gaze instantly zeroed in on her breasts, where the

cami she wore had glued to her skin like an extra layer. A zing of desire shot through her veins.

Not the time.

With a flick of her wrist she twisted her hair up and clamped the cap atop the blond mass.

"They're coming," J.T. muttered as he gazed at some point beyond her.

"Yeah, I know." She planted her palms against the wall on either side of him and leaned in. "Keep your eyes open. Let me know when they're inside."

Then she planted her lips on his.

* * * * *

Will J.T. and Eve be caught in the moment?
Or will Eve get the chance to reveal
all of her secrets?
Find out in
THE BRIDE'S SECRETS
by Debra Webb.
Available August 2009 from Harlequin Intrigue®.

We'll be spotlighting a different series every month throughout 2009 to celebrate our 60th anniversary.

LOOK FOR
HARLEQUIN INTRIGUE®
IN AUGUST!

To commemorate the event, Harlequin Intrigue® is thrilled to invite you to the wedding of the Colby Agency's J.T. Baxley and his bride, Eve Mattson.

Look for *Colby Agency: Elite Reconnaissance*

THE BRIDE'S SECRETS
BY DEBRA WEBB

Available August 2009

www.eHarlequin.com

HIBPA09

REQUEST YOUR FREE BOOKS!

2 FREE NOVELS PLUS 2 FREE GIFTS!

Silhouette® Desire®

Passionate, Powerful, Provocative!

YES! Please send me 2 FREE Silhouette Desire® novels and my 2 FREE gifts (gifts are worth about $10). After receiving them, if I don't wish to receive any more books, I can return the shipping statement marked "cancel". If I don't cancel, I will receive 6 brand-new novels every month and be billed just $4.05 per book in the U.S. or $4.74 per book in Canada. That's a savings of almost 15% off the cover price! It's quite a bargain! Shipping and handling is just 50¢ per book.* I understand that accepting the 2 free books and gifts places me under no obligation to buy anything. I can always return a shipment and cancel at any time. Even if I never buy another book, the two free books and gifts are mine to keep forever.   225 SDN EYMS   326 SDN EYM4

Name	(PLEASE PRINT)	
Address		Apt. #
City	State/Prov.	Zip/Postal Code

Signature (if under 18, a parent or guardian must sign)

Mail to the Silhouette Reader Service:
IN U.S.A.: P.O. Box 1867, Buffalo, NY 14240-1867
IN CANADA: P.O. Box 609, Fort Erie, Ontario L2A 5X3

Not valid to current subscribers of Silhouette Desire books.

Want to try two free books from another line?
Call 1-800-873-8635 or visit www.morefreebooks.com.

* Terms and prices subject to change without notice. Prices do not include applicable taxes. Sales tax applicable in N.Y. Canadian residents will be charged applicable provincial taxes and GST. Offer not valid in Quebec. This offer is limited to one order per household. All orders subject to approval. Credit or debit balances in a customer's account(s) may be offset by any other outstanding balance owed by or to the customer. Please allow 4 to 6 weeks for delivery. Offer available while quantities last.

Your Privacy: Silhouette Books is committed to protecting your privacy. Our Privacy Policy is available online at www.eHarlequin.com or upon request from the Reader Service. From time to time we make our lists of customers available to reputable third parties who may have a product or service of interest to you. If you would prefer we not share your name and address, please check here. ☐

SDES09R

**Stay up-to-date
on all your romance
reading news!**

The Harlequin
Inside Romance
newsletter is a **FREE**
quarterly newsletter
highlighting
our upcoming
series releases
and promotions!

**Go to
eHarlequin.com/InsideRomance**
or e-mail us at
InsideRomance@Harlequin.com
to sign up to receive
your **FREE** newsletter today!

Silhouette Desire

COMING NEXT MONTH
Available August 11, 2009

#1957 BOSSMAN BILLIONAIRE—Kathie DeNosky
Man of the Month
The wealthy businessman needs an heir. His plan: hire his
attractive assistant as a surrogate mother. Her condition: marriage.

**#1958 ONE NIGHT WITH THE WEALTHY RANCHER—
Brenda Jackson**
Texas Cattleman's Club: Maverick County Millionaires
Unable to deny the lingering sparks with the woman he once
rescued, he's still determined to keep his distance…until her life is
once again in danger.

#1959 SHEIKH'S BETRAYAL—Alexandra Sellers
Sons of the Desert
Suspicious of his former lover's true motives, the sheikh sets out
to discover what brought her back to the desert. But soon it's
unclear who's seducing whom….

#1960 THE TYCOON'S SECRET AFFAIR—Maya Banks
The Anetakis Tycoons
A surprise pregnancy is not what this tycoon had in mind after one
blistering night of passion. Yet he insists on marrying his former
assistant…until a paternity test changes everything.

**#1961 BILLION-DOLLAR BABY BARGAIN—
Tessa Radley**
Billionaires and Babies
Suddenly co-guardians of an orphaned baby, they disliked each
other from the start. Until their marriage of convenience flares
with attraction impossible to deny….

#1962 THE MAGNATE'S BABY PROMISE—Paula Roe
This eligible bachelor must marry and produce an heir to keep
the family business. So when he discovers a one-night stand is
pregnant, nothing will get in his way of claiming the baby—and
the woman—as his own.

SDCNMBPA0709